Iadore

&

Ilove

By Mary Hammack

For Paige Rylee

Every word for you!

Part One

Long, Long Ago

Chapter One

A long time ago, deep in the basin of the snowcapped Stolly Mountains lies the beautiful kingdom of Cirlandia. A gentle meandering river divides Cirlandia into two halves, Westland and Eastland. Good King Roland was the 19th ruler in his family's dynasty. Each King passed down their wisdom to the next to maintain the harmony of the kingdom. The only sadness in the land was due to the lack of an heir to the throne and Queen Elena wept every day for want of a child. One bright morning, Queen Elena awoke at feeling somehow different. The royal doctors could not find anything amiss. After 17 years of royal marital bliss, no one even considered the possibility of the Queen being with child but, months later, the Queen blessed the King and kingdom with not only one heir, but two. The first born son was named Prince Roland the 20th. The second was named Prince Richard the 1st, in honor of Queen Elena's father.

The kingdom rejoiced at the birth of the royal twins. Each year following their blessed arrival, the King ordered that a magnificent festival was to be held in their honor. All the knights in the land would compete as in tribute. Each hoped that if they performed well enough, they would gain King's favor. The bakers made birthday cakes for every home. The dress makers made gowns for all the eligible young ladies. The chefs made all the dishes in their cookbooks and would even create a few special dishes for the event. All the citizens in the realm gave what they could to add to the opulence of the festival. Jubilation spread throughout the land.

As the twins grew, once the education tutors completed their lessons for the day, King Roland would then spend a few hours each day teaching Prince Roland all the secrets of being a good monarch and how to maintain the kingdom. During this time Prince Richard would be free to do as he wished. What no one realized was that what Prince Richard truly desired most was his father's throne. Envy grew deep in his heart. Prince Richard would beg and plead with Prince Roland to share their father's lessons. Miserably, having been sworn to secrecy, Prince Roland would have to decline.

A wedge between the twins developed and grew with each passing day. By the time the twins were teenagers, they rarely spoke. Some in the castle even thought the twins were enemies. This concerned Prince Roland deeply and tried repeatedly to make amends. He missed his brother. However, Prince Richard did all he could to nourish his resentment to widen the divide between them. Even though he was the second born son, he knew he was the better heir.

During the festival week of their 16th year, the brothers got into a horrid fight. Prince Richard's resentment had boiled over. The battle between the brothers left them both broken and bruised. In anger over the princes' inability to resolve their conflict peacefully, the King cancelled all future festivals. The realm fell into chaos. Citizens were all taking sides. The kingdom was divided for the first time in its known history. Sadness spread over the land replacing the once peaceful harmony.

Two years later, the sorrow in the land deepened with the tragic death of King Roland. Queen Elena in her grief passed a few days later. Her heart was broken by the loss of her King and the division of her Princes.

Prince Roland became King Roland the 20th. The coronation was a swift, yet low key affair. All were invited, but only a few attended. The citizens all feared retribution for appearing to have taken sides. As his first act as King, King Roland ordered his brother to appear before him and made it mandatory for everyone to bear witness. The throne room was filled with nervous energy. No one knew what the new King was about to do. Would he banish his brother to restore peace?

Prince Richard haughtily sauntered in. The room fell into a deathly silence. King Roland sat upon his throne every bit a proper sovereign. Prince Richard had the look of pure hatred written across his face as he walked up to the throne and begrudgingly knelt to his brother. The air was so still, it seemed that no one even dared to breathe. He would not be accused of disrespecting his brother the way that he himself had been disrespected all his life.

King Roland stood and walked to his brother. He put a gentle hand on his brother's shoulder. Prince Richard started to stand and King Roland slightly shook his head from side to side, keeping his brother on his knees.

"My good people as all of you know our kingdom has been divided by decisions that were made by our beloved father. I am now in a position to make amends to my dear brother. The law of the land has always been that the first born son of the King is to take the throne when the time comes." King Roland eloquently stated after clearing his throat of hesitancy. "My brother has been considered a second class royal, if you will for lack of a better phrase, over a few minutes difference in our age. This is as unacceptable to me as it is to my brother."

Prince Richard's head snaps up in disbelief. What is he doing? Was my brother abdicating the throne for him? It didn't seem possible but the air in the room became thicker still.

"I have decided to share the throne with my brother. It is my decree that we will rule together." King Roland looks at his brother with a smile on his lips and love in his eyes. "Please brother rise and be known as King Richard the 1st hence forth." Slowly, King Richard stands and turns towards some commotion that was occurring behind the throne. Throne was being moved to the side to make room for a second identical throne. Next, to King Richard's surprise, there was to be another coronation ceremony. An identical crown was place on King Richard's head. Tears of righteous joy spilled from his eyes.

"Cherished citizens, I present my brother, my co-ruler, King Richard the 1st". King Roland gave his brother a powerful hug. He whispered in Richard's ear, "I'm sorry brother for all the years you suffered. I was sworn to secrecy by father. This is the way I always thought it should be. I will do all that I can to make up for the past. I have missed you greatly."

The brothers parted. King Richard was speechless, so moved was he by his brother's gesture and words. The room erupted in cheers. Memories of the peaceful realm were flooding everyone's memories. Everyone was full of hope that those days would be coming back. Cirlandia would be restored.

"My second act as King, and I'm confident my brother the King would agree, is to restore the annual festival. We as a kingdom have much to celebrate!" declared King Roland, who looked to see his brother nodding in agreement with enthusiasm.

All these wishful thoughts came to pass. The brothers were happy and closer than ever before. The realm experienced a prosperous peace for many years to come. Until another took first place in King Roland's heart. Isadora.

During the 22nd year at the annual festival, a young lady caught the eye of the Kings. Her beauty was subtle and incomparable to any other maiden in the land. She had a lushness about her that was captivating. Both brothers approached her but she shied away. She confessed to being flattered by their attention but stated clearly that she was no princess or queen. On the last night of the festival during the ball she agreed to one dance with each of the Kings. She danced first with King Richard and then waltzed with King Roland. By the end of that second dance with King Roland she knew she was in love. As it turned out, so was he.

King Roland got down on one knee and asked for her hand in front of everyone. Isadora coyly accepted. The wedding was planned for two weeks hence. The wedding celebration was to be grander than all other festivals combined. The kingdom rejoiced, except King Richard. All his old feelings of resentment returned. He knew he was the better choice of husband. The sour history between the brothers was about to repeat itself.

After the wedding, King Roland had a new idea regarding how to resolve their issues. King Roland proposed that the kingdom be divided. He would rule Westland and King Richard would rule Eastland. King Richard readily agreed. Finally, he will be out from under his brother's shadow. It was his time to shine. He was going to prove to all what he had always known. He *was* the better king.

King Richard's first order of business was to have his Eastlanders build him a castle grander than his brother's. To pay for the castle, he enacted many new tax and labor laws. His citizens, in their unhappiness, tried to move to Westland. This greatly angered King Richard. Clearly, his people lacked vision. He explained that the new laws were only until the castle was built. The people relented. Years went by and the dread and drudgery caused by King Richard's constant demands were never ending. A guarded gate was built on the bridge, preventing any of the Eastlanders from leaving.

Four years into King Richard's reign, the Eastlanders revolted.

King Richard calmed his people by declaring that the cause of all of their pain was Westland. The Westland castle was already built. King Roland *had* everything that was rightfully theirs. He convinced the people of Eastland that the best way out of their current misery was to go to war with Westland and take it all back.

Meanwhile, in Westland, King Roland maintained the peacefulness of his realm using all the lessons taught to him by his father. Westland grew and prospered. He mostly ignored the Eastland troubles. He knew that his brother would not welcome his help or advice. When King Richard declared war on Westland, a piece of King Roland's heart broke forever. He knew there was never going to be a way to appease his brother. He readied his people for the war to come. He shot arrows with messages to the people of Eastland letting them know that he regretted the impending war, apologized for the actions of his brother, and once King Richard was defeated, they would once again be reunited as one Kingdom under his benevolent rule.

The messages sent King Richard into a great rage. He agreed that the kingdom would be under one rule, but it would be his. He vowed that day to kill his brother, King Roland.

Three years later the war continued to drag on. King Roland found Queen Isadora weeping alone in a quiet corner of the castle.

"What saddens my heart so?" King Roland asked, as he sat beside her and gently held her hand.

"A most wonderful thing has happened, my beloved, but it saddens me deeply. At long last I am with child." She cried.

"Oh! What glorious news? Why does our baby make you feel so sad? Is this not what we have both wanted all these years?" King Roland asked with a puzzled look on his face.

"Yes, of course, my beloved. I am sad because our child will be born into a seemingly endless war. I want our child to know the love and peace that we had. I fear that when your brother finds out, he will become even angrier. I have wild imaginings of his reactions. Not one of which are good. What are we to do?" Queen Isadora implored King Roland for any sign that her concerns were unfounded, but she could find none. Once King Roland knew of her concerns, he knew in his heart of hearts that she was right. A new fear gripped him like never before.

Softly, he wiped away her tears. He slowly moved in to give her the Three Kisses. He kissed her left cheek as an unspoken 'I love you endlessly'. He kissed her forehead to replace her fears with the sweetest of dreams. He kissed her right cheek as promise to do all within his ability to ensure her happiness. On their wedding day, King Roland explained the Three Kisses as part of his vows so that she would always know his heart even without words.

"I long to say your fears have no foundation. Alas, I cannot. I share those very fears concerning my brother. I will come up with a solution, I promise you. I will make that a vow to you." King Roland gave each of her hands a sweet kiss. "I will discuss this with my council. I will swear each of them to silence regarding our blessed child. Keeping this to ourselves will give me, us, some time to find a solution." He stood, turned to leave, then looked over his shoulder, and stated, "Please, my dearest heart, shed no more tears over the coming of our beautiful baby. There will be nothing to be distressed about when the time comes. I promise."

The next day King Roland gathered his advisors. Once each man and woman promised his or her silence, the king revealed the news of the royal child and expressed all the concerns that plagued the King and Queen. The announcement was met with cheers of joy and assurances that the situation was well understood. The planning began. Days passed. On the six day, an idea had taken hold of the group.

King Roland sent out scouts to find a new home for all the citizens of Westland. The scouts were to behave like secret agents, telling no one of their mission. Once a new place was found, the move would take place in the dead of night, leaving no trace as to where the Westlanders had gone. King Richard can have everything left behind. The new kingdom will be founded much as Cirlandia was generations ago. Peace and prosperity will once again be the norm for the people, a fresh start with King Richard becoming no more than a cautionary tale.

Weeks went by with no progress. Cirlandia was in the basin of a mountain range that very few could transverse. Those that did explore rarely came back. There was no known passage through the mountains. King Roland knew that since there have been successful expeditions in the past, there had to be a way out. The passageway had to be found. One day during a council meeting, a scout burst into the room shouting that he had a plan.

The scout told the tale of his adventures. The King and council were hanging on his every word. None of them had ever travelled beyond Cirlandia's borders. The scout stated that he had travelled all over the range and did not find a path that he thought all the citizens would be able to traverse. All the routes that he had found were challenging even to him with all his experience. No novices would be able to make the climb safely.

However, he did find a cave. The cave was very large and very deep. He admitted that he did not go very far in but he felt certain that the cave became tunnels that went completely through the mountain. He believed that the cave was large enough to hold all the people of Westland and suggested a caravan to the other side. The cave was located to the west of Westland. On the night of the exodus, it would seem to Eastland that we had just simply disappeared. Then, in order to make sure that none of the Eastlanders could discover where they had gone, he suggested that the cave be closed off with rocks and boulders made to look like a cave in. The only downside to this plan was that this would also mean that no one could ever return.

King Roland ordered that the scout take four of the council members to the cave. Stating that upon their return, a decision would be made. The undertaking was completed. The council members that accompanied the scout agreed with the plan. The cave was huge and very long, cavernous even. There was no reason to question that the plan would work. The move was set to be carried out in a fortnight. The king laid a map of Westland out on the council room table. He divided up the realm into sections. Each council member was responsible for the citizens in their assigned section. Secrecy was of the upmost importance. If word of the plan was learned by any of the Eastlanders, all would be lost. People were only to take what they could carry in a wagon, one wagon per family.

King Richard strolled out onto the balcony of the royal suite one glorious morning. He felt amazing. He felt certain that the war would soon be over with his resounding victory. He searched about, his eyes taking in all the misery within his realm. Then, he begrudgingly glanced to Westland. He did this every day to fuel his hatred and rage, settling his mind on the day's coming battle. This day, however, was different.

He saw nothing of Westland. No people. No livestock. Nothing. His eyes continued to search. He knew something was off, different but he could figure out what it was with the information he was taking in. His mind just could not process what he was seeing.

Suddenly, King Richard sounded the alarm.

"Westland has launched a plot against us!" he yelled. "Prepare for battle! Westland has launched a plot against us! Prepare for battle!" Over and over again, King Richard shouted until everyone was in motion to defend King and kingdom. The army lined up along the river boarder. The gate across the bridge was reinforced. All was in readiness. King Richard was beaming with pride for having spotted the plot and foiled his brother's plans before a single arrow could be fired. Once again proving he was so much smarter than Roland.

Hours passed with nothing happened. Still nothing stirred in Westland. King Richard declared it was a mind game strategy and ordered his people to stand firm. They simply had to wait King Roland out. King Richard knew that King Roland would show his hand at any moment and then the battle would be won before the evil plot could get underway.

Night had come and Westland remained desolate.

Chapter Two

King Roland travelled the length of the caravan. He continually checked on every citizen personally. Congratulating each for their bravery and thanking them for their faith in his leadership. Every night the king collapsed in exhaustion. He felt the true weight of what he had asked his people to risk. This venture had to succeed for the future of all. He vowed to himself that once the people were safe, he would stand down as king if requested for all that he was putting the kingdom through. Queen Isadora understood his burden. She knew that it was his burden to carry, but experienced a deep sense of guilt for having caused it. She felt responsible for everyone else's suffering on journey. If not for her and the royal baby, the Westlanders would still be in their comfortable homes surrounded by the familiar.

The people, nonetheless, understood the need for King Roland's plan and were eager for it. They had grown tired of the war and all of King Richard's antics. All of this was expressed to the King and Queen to ease their fears and apprehension. Yes this was a bold venture but when thinking about new land and the harmonious future, the asking price was worth paying. There was not a hint of doubt in any one's heart. King Roland and Queen Isadora tried to believe in the sincerity of their people, but felt no relief.

The caravan had been travelling for weeks with no end in sight. Moods were starting to dampen. The King continued his daily routine of keeping in touch with each citizen. The Queen was really starting to show the growth of the royal child she carried. The people rejoiced at the sight of her and were more committed than ever to help King Roland secure their future. Their faith in this quest never wavered. They knew King Roland's intentions were true.

One day a scout came running from the front of the line exclaiming that he had found a grotto large enough for the caravan to set up a make shift camp. There was even a rivulet of fresh water. It was a good place for everyone to get some much needed rest. He offered to continue to search for a way out of the mountain while the people recovered. The King told him no. He had recognized the scout as the very same man that found the cave that started it all.

"You my friend have done so much in service of the realm. You, more than anyone else, deserves this respite. Please, honor the Queen and me with your company for dinner this night." King Roland said with a smile.

That night, the cavern was full of life. People were laughing. Shelters were made for privacy. All delighted in knowing that the travelling was done for a time. Fires were lit. Food was being shared throughout the community. A sense of joy was felt once again. No one paid any attention to the bits of light on the walls of the cavern, lights of every color in the rainbow.

A week had passed. During this time, King Roland had been all over the cavern, checking each nook and cranny of the space thoroughly for his self. He, subsequently, had another idea to present to his people.

"My good people, I have called you all together so that each of you could have an opportunity to speak. I no longer believe that the decisions for the many should be made by the few. Words fail me when I attempt to express my gratitude for all that you have sacrificed for what I believed was in the best interests of the realm. I am humbled by your continued faith in my ability to lead." King Roland addressed the crowd with an unassuming demeanor. "I have personally explored the cavern. I have determined that with the amount of food that we have stored and a source of fresh, clean water, we have all that we need to sustain us for many more months. I would like to propose that we stay here for a while longer or until the Queen delivers. I know it will be challenging. Without the torches, the cavern has no natural source of light. Yet, I think we would all benefit from the rest. Once the Queen has recovered, we can then continue our journey. How say you?"

Murmurs rose from the crowd as the people talked among themselves. The King patiently waited. He was willingly at their mercy. He noticed one of the men moving amid the crowd, conversing briefly with each small group. King Roland watched and assumed that this man was a going to be a spokesperson for the community. This thought was confirmed when the man stepped to the front of the crowd to speak to the King.

"Your Royal Highness," the man stated as he bowed deeply, "I have spoken to many here. The general consensus is to remain, but we want you to know that this is not just for the sake of the Queen and your child. We are all a bit weary of travelling and have found some comfort here. We agree that there will be many challenges. We thank you for asking us. No king has ever consulted us, the common people, before that any of us can remember. This only strengthens our belief in you. The sacrifices that you yourself have willingly made and the concern you have shown each of us is unlike anything we have ever experienced."

Once again, the man bowed. He has never spoken to a royal person, much less a king, before. He just hoped that he was not making a fool of himself. "We also agree to revisit the issue of continuing the journey when Queen Isadora is sure that she is ready for travel. We recognize this journey must have been trying for her as well. We are and remain your true citizens." He gave one last bow to signify that he had finished.

"Dear gentleman, what is your name?" King Roland asked.

"I am no one of consequence, Your Majesty, but, ah, my name is Arlen." He said with a shrug.

"You are mistaken, Arlen. You are very much a man of consequence." stated the King. "I observed you taking the initiative to be a spokesman for the people and so you shall be. You have shown me that I require such a person. For this, I owe you many thanks. I have just this moment decided that my council is in need of a new member. I wish to welcome you to the King's Council. All hail Arlen, King's Spokesman for the People." The crowd gasped as King Roland bowed to Arlen.

The crowd erupted in cheers. Men came by to clap the stunned Arlen on the back in congratulations. Slowly, Arlen raised his hand for silence.

"I am honored, your Majesty and I accept if you are sure. I know not what I can contribute or why after all this time you think a Spokesman is needed." questioned Arlen. "You are indeed needed, Sir Arlen. As I stated before, I and my council have asked much of all of you. I cannot express with any kind of accuracy what your fellowship has meant to me. You followed me, us," King Roland gestured to include Queen Isadora and the other council members, "in faith.

"I only hope that each of you know how truly dedicated I am to providing for my kingdom and to keeping us all safe from war. I want to present opportunities of growth. I want us all to find the harmony that we once cherished." King Roland paused. "From now on, I will only remain your King if you, the people, wish it. All decisions that affect us all will be made by us all. Each will have an equal say. I would like to suggest a majority rule in lieu of a unanimous rule. I have a council man to advise me on commerce. I have a council woman to advise me on the health. I have a council man to advise me on defense and safety. I have council for each area of rule.

Up until now, we, the council and I, made decisions and all of you just had to accept whatever we decided. The undertaking of leaving everything behind in search of a new home has opened my eyes to the unfairness of the current system. I will not ask of my people to follow me blindly, regardless of how willing, any longer. You, Sir Arlen, have shown me how to get the thoughts of the people into the council room. In addition, as my dearest heart, Queen Isadora gets closer to the arrival of our child; I am becoming more and more reluctant to leave her side. I will be most grateful to you, Arlen, and the other council members for allowing me the opportunity to be there for the Queen.

"I very much want to be there to welcome our child into the world. I want to be a witness to the birth. I no longer want to be a hands off monarch. I beseech you to trust in the sincerity of my words." King Roland gave this impassioned speech in front of all he ruled. Never before had a King behaved in this way. All were moved. A few shed a tear or two.

"Your Majesty, forgive me. You are only asking for what each of us takes for granted. I am ashamed to admit that I have never before considered the sacrifices a king must make for his people. I have always done my best to serve the kingdom just by being a good citizen. Today, I vow to serve you in this and any manner you ask." Arlen cleared his throat and then addressed the crowd. "I have settled my family in this tent." He pointed to the third tent on the right side. "Please come to me with any thoughts or concerns. I have pledged to serve the king and all of you. I feel honored to serve. I truly believe a new kingdom has, in fact, been founded on this day." This time Arlen bowed to the crowd displaying his respect for them all.

Applause thundered in the cavern. The bits of light that no one seemed to notice began to grow brighter and larger to the amazement of the cheering people. Some even mistakenly thought that the lights were somehow arranged by King Roland as a way to celebrate the decision to remain in the cavern.

No one could have guessed what was about to happen.

Chapter Three

As the lights grew, shapes began to form within the bright centers. The shapes became people. The lights faded revealing that they were surrounded by a luminous people. The Westlanders slowly began to notice differences between the light people and themselves. Most noticeable, their skin glowed a bit in shades of every color and they had wings.

Quiet filled the cavern as both groups stared at the other. The silence was heavy.

"I am Queen Gemeenah and this is my kingdom. My fairies and I have been watching all of you since your arrival. Please tell me why it is that you had to flee from your home? How is it that you all have come to be here?" She addressed King Roland, who remained speechless. He could only stare in disbelief. "Come now. I know you are their King."

Queen Gemeenah was resplendent. While all the fairies were of one color, she had pale skin mottled with many colors. Her long straight white hair fell to the ground. The hair on her right side was casually tucked behind a pointed ear. Her eyes were the brightest shade of green that Roland had ever seen. He realized that she was speaking to him but her lips never moved. Her words were clear only in his head. He quickly glanced around to see if anyone else had heard her but was unable to tell. Patiently, she looked at him with a questioning look. As if she was asking again with her eyes.

"I'm-m-m-m s-s-s-s-sorry…" King Roland stammered. "D-did you say fairies?"

Queen Gemeenah made no reply, just continued with her questioning stare, flexing her wings to point out the obvious.

King Roland managed to pull himself together enough to tell the Queen Gemeenah the history of Cirlandia and the tragedy of his brother, King Richard. He explained that when he realized that his Queen was living in fear of what his brother would do in retaliation to the news of the royal child, the time to leave had come. Queen Isadora and he had grown tired of war and could no longer tolerate his brother's unpredictable antics. He was sure that if the Royal family were weary of what had become of Cirlandia, then his people must be as well. He told her the whole tale, pouring his heart out to her. He told her of the desire of his family and his people to find a new home, to once again live in peace and harmony. The current plan was to leave again once Queen Isadora had recovered. Then, it dawned on him that he was rambling, not explaining their presence in the cavern. He blushed and threw a hand over his mouth.

Amused, Queen Gemeenah could not prevent a tiny giggle from escaping. The sound was magical. She had tried so hard to appear fierce and stern. This time she spoke out loud to the Westlanders. "Are all of you in agreement with quest for a new home?" She searched the crowd. There were a few dazed nods but still all were silent.

"Ahem. I am Sir Arlen. I am Spokesman for the People of Westland. Yes, Your Grace, all that our King has said is true. I offer our apologies for invading your kingdom, as we did not know of you." King Roland was astonished. Arlen was absolutely the right man.

Queen Gemeenah nodded slowly, walking casually about. "I see" was all she said. King Roland could tell that she was deep in thought. He was aching inside to know what she was thinking but feared to interrupt. He anxiously waited for her to be the one to break the silence.

Abruptly, she looked at King Roland and declared I must speak to you privately. With the snap of her fingers all the fairies were made light and gone. Queen Isadora screamed when she realized that King Roland had also vanished. The Westlanders gasped. Several of the ladies rushed to Queen Isadora's side in fear that she would faint.

Queen Gemeenah could be heard, but not seen, saying "My apologies. Fear not. I'll return him in a bit. We just have much to discuss. Please be at ease fair lady." Everyone looked about to see where the voice was coming from. Eventually, they came to understand that it was some sort of fairy magic. Queen Isadora sighed a bit with relief, but still worried about her Roland. She did love him so.

King Roland found himself in what appeared to be Queen Gemeenah's sitting room. It was elegantly decorated with flowers, but the room was not overly lavish. Then he noticed that the room was not decorated with flowers, but the furnishings were flowers. He stood still, not knowing what else to do. He had no experience with other royals from other kingdoms much less of another race.

"Sit. Sit" Queen Gemeenah voicelessly said. Roland thought this was going to take some getting used to.

"You'll get used to it sooner than you think."

King Roland was stunned when he realized not only could he hear her in his head, she could read his thoughts. Panic raced through his mind trying to see what else he might have thought that she had heard and hoping none of it was offensive.

Queen Gemeenah giggled again.

"What a remarkable creature you are! Do you always worry so much about others?"

"I am a King, your Grace. Service to others is all I know." He offered with a slight bow.

"Interesting." Queen Gemeenah sat reflectively.

"Is it? Do you have much experience with humans? I confess I thought fairies were only stories of wishful thinking made up to entertain children. May I ask how it is that we, humans I mean, do not know of your existence? Is this planned? I have a thousand questions racing through my mind, but do not wish to overwhelm you with a barrage of questions." He said earnestly.

"Honestly, my fairies and I have always known about humans. We intentionally stayed away. We have heard many a cautionary tales about humans. Nothing that we had come to believe about humans seems to be true from what we have learned from watching all of you. I too have many, many questions."

Roland thought to himself, well what an interesting situation I have found myself in. He sat down on one of the lush yellow rhododendron pillows that were scattered about the room. He did not see any chairs. He jostled around a bit until he found a comfortable way to sit on a flower. Shaking his head a little, he was still unable to wrap his mind around what was happening. No use denying it, he told himself. You are not delusional. No accident or head injury. He pinched his leg. Ouch! Does that mean that I'm awake?

Queen Gemeenah watched... and listened. She was completely amused by him in every way. She had always believed that humans were a horrible greedy, selfish race. Her fairies did not find any of this to be true. The Westlanders were observed to be kind to one another. They shared all that they had willingly. What a delightful mystery?

"Would you care for some refreshment?" she interrupted his musings to ask. He simply nodded, but he thought why not. This cannot be really happening.

She handed him a white daylily flower for a cup full of a thick clear liquid with a hint of a smile.

"This is wildflower nectar. This batch was harvested yesterday morning. It's still tastes fresh. Do your people like to drink nectar?" she wondered.

"I do not believe we have the ability to harvest wildflower nectar." Roland took a sip and his eyes grew wide. "Wow! Nectar is really sweet and the most delicious drink I have ever tasted. Not even our finest wines come close to this. Does nectar have any *effect* on the drinker?"

"Effect? What do you mean?" She looked in his mind and saw some flashes of happy staggering people Roland had seen at the festivals over the years. "Oh, I see what you mean and no, not that I am aware of. Though, I am speaking of fairies not humans."

"Actually, that is good. I can honestly say that I have never been as you saw in my mind. I mean, of course, I have plenty of wine in my day, but my father always said to remember who I am. No one will follow a drunken King that is a laughing buffoon." She did not entirely understand what he was saying but thought she understood the sentiment. "May I have some more, please. I promise to drink this one more slowly." He said with a smile.

"Of course. Please, make yourself at home. We have much to talk about. I would very much like to get to know you and your people better. I believe we can work something out for our collective futures."

They talked and laughed for hours.

Chapter Four

Queen Isadora did faint. She had continued to worry about King Roland and his absence. She became thoroughly distraught. Until she just seemed to give out. The ladies that had rushed to her side asked a few of the men to carry her inside. The ladies gathered around their Queen. They were doing all that they could to comfort and revive her. Almost without notice, a fairy had quietly entered the royal tent. A hush fell upon the group as a light purple hand, long and elegant, reached out to touch Queen Isadora's forehead. One of the Westland ladies moved to stop her, but the rest held her back. There was a questioning look on all of their faces. None sensed that the fairy woman had meant any harm. When her hand made contact with the Queen, her fingertips glowed and the fairy closed her eyes. The Queen relaxed, but remained unconscious.

After a moment, the fairy greeted the group.

"Hello. My name is Violet. I noticed your Queen was distressed and only wished to help." She said. Her voice had a sweet musical quality. "I spoke to her. I assured her that neither she nor any of you have to fear us. It is not in our nature to be unkind to any other living beings. I also spoke to the child within. She is beautiful and strong. I look forward to meeting her and watching her grow. Humans and fairies are very different in this way. We have fairy light that allows us to live for centuries. We rarely have young ones. This little one is already full of spirit and adventure. She will bring us all great joy."

"What do you mean you will watch her grow? Are you keeping us here?" The woman that moved to stop Violet questioned with alarm in her voice.

"No." Violet replied with a small smile. "I know this is all very new to you. I am sure that none of you were even aware of the existence of fairies. You probably thought us to be only make believe. That is by our doing. Many, many years ago, fairies and humans lived to together. The humans became greedy and selfish. They demanded more and more from the magical peoples. It seemed that the humans were never satisfied. I know now that not all humans are this way, but the situation became very hard for magical folk. A gathering was held and a decision was made. A divide was created between humans and the magical peoples."

"Peoples? What else is there? And what do you mean that the humans became greedy and selfish. What happened?" the woman demanded. "Oh, I'm sorry. I do not mean for my questions to come out like accusations. My name is Vera and I'm terribly curious about all of this. I thought I knew much of our history as a race, but I confess I know nothing of what you speak."

Violet bowed to Vera ever so slightly and again she smiled. "No need to apologize. As I mentioned, this gap in your histories was by design. Shall we step outside? We will leave your Queen to rest and I will answer all that I can."

The rest of the Westlanders had been waiting anxiously to hear about what was happening in the royal tent. All those standing outside the royal tent had witnessed Violet enter the tent uninvited. Imaginations were running wild. No one could picture what was happening in there.

Vera looked for Arlen. She wanted to catch him up so that he could inform the rest.

"Arlen. This is Violet. She eased Queen Isadora's mind so that she could rest. She has offered to answer any questions that we have. She has much to tell us. I thought with your new role it should be you to introduce her and assure everyone that we have nothing to fear. We should listen." Vera stated clearly, as if she were no longer surprised by any of this.

Cautiously, Arlen stepped up on the natural platform of dirt and turned to face the crowd. He was no longer feeling as confident about talking in front of a large group. Nerves took him. Violet laid a soft hand on his forearm. A warm glow seemed to spread to Arlen's arm. His head jerked up to face Violet. She responded with a nod and a smile.

"Hey, um, this is Violet. She has much to tell us." Arlen stammered out even though he was comforted by Violet, he was still at a loss for words. There was nothing he could say that the people could not see for themselves.

"I understand that the discovery of our existence is quite a surprise and perhaps a bit of a shock to all of you. I know there are many questions. I have promised to answer all that I can. Let me first say that there is nothing to fear here. There is nothing and no one here that will cause any harm." Violet glanced over her shoulder to look at Vera. "I have started to share our story with the others but I wish to start over so that all can know." Violet waved her hand and a dirt pile rose in the shape of a stool. The crowd gasped and Violet casually sat down. "I did not mean to cause alarm. There is so much for us to learn about one another."

Violet repeated what she had said in the royal tent. "Vera has already asked some questions. I would like to start by answering her questions again. Yes. I did say peoples. There are fairies, dwarves, giants, and all manner of magical people. I had learned long ago that the humans were greedy and selfish. Humans were not to be trusted. I have learned from watching all of you, this is not true. As you all just witnessed fairies have the ability to control all things in nature. I was able to move the earth to make myself a seat, for example. Dwarves mined gold and gems that the humans valued. Giants could clear trees from large areas with a few swipes of their hands. The humans demanded that fairies use magic to make crops grow more quickly and more plentiful. They took what the dwarves mined with nothing in return. The humans wanted more and more forest cleared to increase their crops to be able to maintain their ever growing kingdoms. The humans lived in excess wanting everything done for them by the magical folks instead of doing for themselves. At the gathering, the magical folk decided to remove ourselves from the human realms. Humans must learn to live on their own without the use of magic. It was felt by us that humans lacked the respect that nature and magic required."

The Westlanders remained quiet. They listened with intensity to all that Violet had to say. Questions were shouted and she calmly replied. This went on for hours. The meeting between Queen Gemeenah and King Roland was all but forgotten. It was an enjoyable event of learning. A light started to fall from the top of the cavern and settled on the platform by Violet. Queen Gemeenah and King Roland stood off to the side of Violet.

"Whew! That is certainly going to take some time to get used to." King Roland said with a laugh.

Queen Gemeenah giggled in response and then inquired of Violet what was happening here.

"My Queen, I sensed the alarm the disappearance of their leader caused these good people. Their Queen collapsed and I wished to comfort them." Violet stated to explain herself.

Upon hearing the Queen Isadora had collapsed King Roland was gripped with fear and started searching for her with his eyes. "King Roland, please, be at ease. She is resting in the tent. I relaxed her mind so that she could rest. I also spoke to your child. I am so looking forward to embracing her. What a delight she is!" Violet quietly exclaimed.

King Roland paused and looked at Violet. His mind was buzzing with all that Violet had just said. How could she comfort my unconscious wife? What does she mean by embracing her? Are we having a girl? How can she speak to an unborn child? So many questions raced around his mind, but no words came out. He was unmoving in place. All he could do was look inquiringly at Violet. Then he got an amused expression on his face and shot his eyes in the direction of Queen Gemeenah. With a slight nod he seemed to accept the information. He fought his urge to run to his Queen, trusting in Violet's words. He spoke to his people instead.

"Queen Gemeenah has offered to share this cavern with us until my beloved has recovered from the arrival of our roy... hmm...a... our daughter." With that he acknowledged Violet, who nodded in reply. "We can then decide if we wish to remain here or continue with our journey. I know that we as a community have already made this decision, but we must concede that we are not alone here. I am overwhelmed and overjoyed with Queen Gemeenah's generous offer. I sincerely hope that this is all good and well with all of you. If any of you wish to leave now, and not wait for the Princess," This felt so odd for King Roland to say. "Queen Gemeenah has offered scouts to lead those of you who wish to leave threw the mountain to the other side. Please do not rush to answer but discuss with your families. We all must do what we believe to be in the best interests for ourselves. I would like to add that I have the deepest hope that we will remain united." King Roland bowed his departure.

King Roland sat on the bed next to his Queen, taking her hand into his. Gently, he moved tresses of her dark lush hair from her face. She stirred and murmured, but did not wake. The pair remained this way for a time. Queen Isadora was lost in her dreams. King Roland was lost in his thoughts.

Meanwhile, on the raised area outside, Queen Gemeenah was fielding questions from the Westlanders. She reassured the people as much as she could that they were not prisoners of the fairy kingdom. She expressed that she had no doubt that they could all learn from one another and live accordingly. They were welcome to plant gardens and make homes in the spacious cavern.

"Grow gardens? In a cave? There is no sunlight, Your Highness. I appreciate your offer but I do not believe that we will be able to survive here once our supplies run out." Shouted a man from the crowd.

"Oh, yes, of course!" Queen Gemeenah waved her hand about the cavern. Color exploded everywhere the eye could see. Giant citrines were above lit up the entire grotto with gemlight. The torches that had been placed all around went out. Flowers of every kind and color could be seen in every direction. The stream that went through the center of the cavern bubbled with fish. Trees grew in clusters with branches heavy with gorgeous, ripe fruit, all kinds of fruit. The Westlanders found that they were in a land of abundance.

"Much to learn my new friends," she chuckled and disappeared. "Much to learn." Could be heard echoing through the air at her leaving.

The Westlanders immersed themselves in life in the cavern. Everyone had chosen to stay. A rhythm had settled among both races. They shared all that they could and delighted in learning each other's ways. Weeks had passed. The wonders of the cavern never ceased to amaze the humans. The citrines grew slowly bright in the morning and dimmer as the day ended, mimicking day and night seamlessly. During the night, the cavern ceiling sparkled with thousands of smaller gems. The nighttime ceiling appeared as a spray of multicolored stars. The fairies had homes within the cavern walls. Holes of varying size could be made into a fairy home with a little magic. Many of the gem stars were actually fairy homes. It was a thrilling and mystical time for both groups.

Chapter Five

An anguished scream ripped through the cave. Queen Isadora was bringing the royal babe into world. The pain was horrible. She has heard every mother say this and now she knew the truth of it. She tried to comfort herself with the other words the mothers had shared with her. All the pain would be forgotten once she held her child. King Roland was by her side. The midwives were busy making the Queen as comfortable as possible. All the preparations had been made. Queen Gemeenah and Violet appeared in the royal tent. She asked King Roland to leave and requested the two midwives to stay.

Violet spoke to the women, not knowing which of the two was in charge.

"Something is wrong with the Queen. The infant is in much distress, please allow us to help."

Sarah and Susan were sister midwives. They have served the royal family all their lives. They even chose to serve the royal family of Cirlandia over having families of their own. Sarah, the older of the two, took the lead.

"This is common among our people. Bringing a child into the world is very painful. We expected this since it is her first child." Sarah offered.

"No." Queen Gemeenah took over for Violet. "We mean that the Queen will not survive. Remember, kind lady, we have a magical relationship to all things in nature. Child birth is natural. We can feel the infant's pain. The Queen is very weak. She will deliver the princess but not live to hold her. We have come to ease her passing. She need not suffer with this pain."

"I will not allow you to harm our Queen!" shouted Susan.

Queen Isadora screamed once more and passed out.

"It is too late for your Queen. You will need to take the princess from her. Do it quickly or you will lose the princess as well." Violet shouted back.

Sarah and Susan realized the truth in what the fairies were saying. Grief gripped them both. They stood Unmoving and staring at their beautiful queen. The women were already reeling from the loss.

"Now! You must act now!" Queen Gemeenah's cried out and snapped the sisters into action. Carefully, Sarah took the baby from the queen. Tears rolled down her cheek and fell on to the baby.

"A princess just as you said. I'm sorry I didn't believe. I know… I have much to learn." Sarah whispered.

"What are we to tell the King?" Susan wondered aloud.

All were silent except for the baby. Her crying had calmed to a soft whimper. The women knew of the deep love King Roland had for Queen Isadora. All feared his reaction. They did not fear that he would be angry. They feared he would be consumed by grief. They feared for the baby. All were worried that he would blame the child for taking away his Queen.

"Take the princess with you. Give her all the love and care that her mother would have. Keep her until I come for her. Violet, please tend to Queen Isadora. King Roland must not see her this way. I will speak with King Roland." Queen Gemeenah seemed to know exactly what needed to be done. Every one obeyed without question, grateful that she took charge.

Violet had quickly washed Queen Isadora and dressed her in a clean gown. She changed the bedding. She now appeared to be angelically sleeping. Sarah and Susan had left with the princess to do the same for her. The princess was given a bath and dressed in a beautiful soft ivory colored lace gown. The sight of her was breathtaking as she slept in her bassinette. With the necessary duties done, they patiently waited for Queen Gemeenah's return.

Queen Gemeenah dreaded what had to be done next but knew to delay would be cruel. King Roland was pacing in front of the tent. He had heard the princess cry out. He could not wait to kiss his beloved Queen. His arms ached to hold their daughter. He smiled at the thought, "I have a daughter!" One look at Queen Gemeenah's face and his heart sank. He knew something was terribly wrong but could not conceive of what it could be. He took the hand that she had extended to him and let her lead him into the tent. His eyes swelled with tears at the sight of his love. She was so beautiful, even as she slept he thought to himself.

"I am very sorry for your loss. I am here for whatever you need." Queen Gemeenah said barely above a whisper. She faded from sight leaving King Roland alone with his wife for the last time.

At first King Roland was confused by Queen Gemeenah's words. He went to Queen Isadora. He sat down gently, not wanting to wake her. He took her hand as he always has.

"My sweet beloved, you have done it! Our daughter is here. I heard her healthy cry. She is with the midwives I guess but I cannot wait to hold her. I know I will see your beauty in her face." He spoke so softly. Then, he furrowed his brow as he realized that her hand was cold. "You are so cold my love." Wrapping his other hand around the one he held. It was then that he noticed that Queen Isadora breathed no more. His mind tried to deny what he knew in his heart to be true. At first, he whimpered in effort to try to control and sort his emotions. He lost all control in moments. The sound of his sobs filled the cavern. All knew what had become of Queen Isadora before the announcement was made.

All of the Westlanders fell into deep mourning, wailing all day and all night. None could get a grip on their sorrow. The fairies were at a loss as to how to help their new friends. Even Queen Gemeenah behaved strangely. She seemed to act as if the death of Queen Isadora was somehow her fault. No one could understand what she was feeling or thinking. All she would say is that her heart ached for King Roland and his people. After two days of intense grief had passed, the time to take some action had come.

Queen Gemeenah entered the royal tent where Queen Isadora still laid, beautiful as ever. King Roland had not left her side nor had he let go of her hand. Queen Gemeenah gasped in order to stifle her own cries of grief at the sight of them. Violet was behind her holding the nameless princess. The fairies had been taking care of her with the help of Susan and Sarah. The royal baby was bundled snuggly within a plush pink blanket. Sweet daisies had been decoratively woven in to it. She was such a sweet sight.

"Ahem." Queen Gemeenah softly interrupted King Roland's reverie. He glanced up at her but never truly changed his focus. Queen Isadora held his full attention as much now as she had on the day that they met all those years ago. "King Roland, I am sorry but it is time. Your people need you. More importantly, your daughter needs you. She also needs a name."

King Roland acknowledged the words she had spoken, but still kept his focus on his beloved. Queen Gemeenah looked to Violet with her arms outstretched. Violet gently handed her the royal baby. She cradled her sweetly with one arm. She used the other arm to force King Roland to look at her. His eyes grew wide as if he had completely forgotten about the princess, his daughter. Fresh tears spilled from his eyes in shame for having neglected the child he had so wanted just two days prior.

Closing his eyes, he sobbed. "Please take her away. I am not worthy of her."

"Nonsense! Your wound is deep in your heart. However, as I said, the time has come." Queen Gemeenah was firm yet caring. Slowly, she helped King Roland to his feet and handed him the child. With shaking arms and tender hands, King Roland held his daughter for the first time. He sobbed again, but this time, his tears were of love and joy. He marveled at every aspect of her. She was, to his eyes, perfect in every way.

"Oh! I never imagined I could feel this much love for another person. Is it possible that she is even more beautiful than her mother?" A smile broke across King Roland's face. For the second time in his life, he was completely smitten. This time, it was with his daughter.

"What shall we call her? Did you have a name picked out?" Violet asked. Queen Gemeenah dared not speak. She was so moved watching King Roland. The affection and delight radiated off of him in waves, filling the room. She knew that she would lose what little control she had over her own emotions if she tried to talk.

"No, not really. We talked about many names and we could never agree." King Roland chuckled at this admission. "Oh my!" He said looking at his daughter. "What is your name to be? I adore you already beyond all words!" After a moment, he exclaimed, "That's it. Welcome to the world Princess Iadore." He gave fleeting look to Queen Gemeenah. "Princess Iadore Daisy."

King Roland knew that the fairy folk always took their names from nature. He did not know where the precious blanket had come from but he wanted to honor the fairies and the person who gifted his daughter with the blanket. Queen Gemeenah immediately understood the gesture. She could no longer contain her tears. She let them flow freely.

"Let us introduce her to the rest of the realm." She murmured.

Chapter Six

King Roland stepped out of the royal tent. Princess Iadore tucked safely in the cradle of his arm. He looked out at the crowd. Pride, joy, love, so many feelings just seemed to roll off of him in an emotional wave that washed over all who had gathered.

"I must first apologize for my lack of leadership of the last few days. I am your King, but as you can see, I am also human. As all of you know, I deeply loved our Queen." He muffled a sob. "The loss of her is devastating to me. I ask that you try to channel your streams of grief into rivers of love. I want to introduce you all to my daughter. Princess Iadore Daisy. I hope that you all embrace her." He held her up just a touch to show her to the crowd. "Before this day, I had thought that there was no greater love than my love for Queen Isadora. Today, I know a stronger love exists. It is the love of a father for his daughter."

King Roland was quiet for a few moments before continuing.

"Tomorrow we will have two ceremonies. The first will be a Good Bye ceremony for my beloved Queen Isadora. We shall all grieve together one last time. We will share our memories of her. We, as a people, will lay her to rest in the peace." He paused for a moment to let the solemnity to settle. "The second ceremony will be a Welcome Blessing ceremony for Princess Iadore Daisy. Let us all welcome her and express all our well wishes for her happiness. The day will begin in sadness and end with happiness. In the old days of Cirlandia, our kingdom held a festival each year to celebrate the arrival of my brother and I. Sadly, for many reasons, we have not had much to celebrate in recent years. This changes as of now! We will once again enjoy annual festivals."

The Westlanders in the crowd cheered. They felt that the King was keeping his promise to find a new home and to bring back the days of yore. Princess Iadore cemented the fragile new community together. The fairies were a bit confused by the King's words. They had no knowledge of the ceremonies and festivals that he had described. However, this did not prevent the fairies from being swept up in the joyous tide that was moving through the cavern.

That night Queen Gemeenah worked with the King Roland and his council to make sure that all the preparations for the ceremonies was made. She also wanted to learn more about the ceremonies and the festival. Queen Gemeenah had become very fond of the humans. She remembered that the original agreement was to let the people stay in the cavern until the arrival of Princess Iadore. Now, she privately worried that once the ceremonies and the festival were done, the humans would leave to continue on their original journey.

The humans had come to love life with the fairies. Many of the Westlanders had the same concerns. No one wanted to bother King Roland during this emotional time. There was naught to do, but wait.

When the citrine sun began to shine in the morning, every one, human and fairy, came out for the first ceremony. Queen Isadora was wrapped in big leaves entwined with wild flower vines. The vines crisscrossed up her body and then formed a crown of flowers. Her face was serenely beautiful. She was the very picture of restful sleep. The fairies watched the humans to see how to behave and what to expect. The Westlanders came by Queen Isadora one by one. Each stopped by her side. Some spoke out loud while others just knelt with silent tears. The fairies observed all this and understood the meaning of the ceremony. Very few of the fairy folk got the opportunity to meet Queen Isadora but all could feel how much the Westlanders loved her.

This caused the fairies to love her as well. Once all the humans had made their farewells, the fairies followed suit. Each expressed what was in his or her heart. King Roland was moved by the fairies honoring a Queen that was not theirs. He marveled at their capacity to care so much for someone new to their community. When all had been said and all the tears had been dried, Queen Isadora was moved to a grassy spot close to but not quite under an apple tree. Apples were her favorite fruit. The Counselors gently laid her down on the grass. Queen Gemeenah moved her left hand and the earth slowly moved over Queen Isadora as if to swallow her. Then she slowly waved her right hand over the place when she had lain and wild flowers erupted to mark her place of honorable rest. King Roland blew out a white candle that was burning on the platform in the center of the cavern. The first ceremony of the day was done.

The rest of the citrine day was spent in hushed solitude.

With the onset of gem night, humans and fairies came out to celebrate the birth of Princess Iadore Daisy. She was in a bassinette on the platform in the center of the village wearing a white lace gown decorated with daisies. Queen Gemeenah had a little crown made of gold, silver, and gemstone daisies crafted as a festival day gift for the princess. King Roland accepted the gift with great humility. Queen Gemeenah and King Roland had become very close friends. Each cherished the kindness and wisdom of the other. It was a unique bond unlike anything either had experienced before. It was a kind of love, but not romantic love. As rulers, there were experiences and feelings that only they could understand. This shared understanding only deepened their friendship.

"You are too generous, my friend." King Roland said, in amazement of the delicate beauty of the crown.

"Not at all, King Minegard owed me a favor." She replied off handedly.

"Who?" King Roland asked with a bemused look on his face.

"Oh! I sometimes forget how new all this is to you still. King Minegard is the ruler of one of the nearby Dwarf Clans. He has a taste for our wildflower nectar. I make sure he has just enough to wet his appetite and he keeps the other Dwarf Clans away from our cavern. We also occasionally do favors for one another. His people are true masters of craft. When I explained what I had in mind for Princess Iadore, he readily agreed. This lovely crown far exceeds anything that I could have imagined. I am certain he will want to meet with you and your people. Would you be open to that?" Queen Gemeenah explained all this without taking her eyes off of Princess Iadore. All who looked upon her fell under her spell or so it would seem. King Roland was lost in thought. She always provided so much information and so casually that it left him a bit speechless. Finally, he resolved that this type of situation was just something he was going to have to accept.

With a big smile on his face he replied, "I would be very much pleased to meet King Min...what did you call him?"

"King Minegard." She smiled back. "I will let him know when it would be a good time to come. He is quite intrigued by the fact that we are choosing to live together. We are making that choice, are we not? I am angered with myself for asking to be honest. I was trying to not pry. I know that our original agreement was for you and your people to stay until after the babe had arrived, but you see, we have all become quite fond of all of you. I wish for you to consider this as you meet with your council for your final decision."

"Allow me to ease your worries now. I very much would like to remain. I still have to discuss this with my council and people. That is how I promised to rule. I also confess my fondness for you and your people. I also believe that my daughter will have a greatly enriched life being raised here. I cannot imagine that I could find a better place for us to live." He had a sparkle in his eye as he spoke. "I plan to meet with my council the day after tomorrow. I think all would benefit from a day of rest after all that is happening today."

Queen Gemeenah gave a knowing smile and was pleased with his response to her concerns. The Westlanders were free to stay or go. "Well then, let us begin with the Welcome Blessing. Sarah explained the ceremony to us. I look forward to it. I thank you for including us."

"Of course. I intended for all our events to be jointly celebrated going forward." King Roland stated decisively. Even though the two rulers agreed to make decisions together, this one he made himself and knew it would be unquestioningly accepted. He was right.

Exiting the tent to address the crowd, King Roland held up Princess Iadore. For many, this was the first time seeing the royal baby. The cavern filled with sounds of "Oh", "Ah", and gasps of pleasant surprise.

"Oh my, look how beautiful she is!"

"She has the look of her mother!

"Bless the babe!"

King Roland moved to cradle Princess Iadore with one hand as he raised his other hand to silence the crowd.

He looked around the cavern, taking in all the faces, fairy and human.

"Normally I would begin my speech with "My good people..." but as I look around I am reminded that we have come to a new kingdom. We have found another race of people that have welcomed us, made a place for us. A place that we can make our new home. I can think of no better place to raise my daughter. I look around and all I can see is love peering back. I am so grateful to all of you for following me on this journey."

King Roland continued. "When we set out I could not have imagined a place such as this. I am also grateful for the magical life my daughter will have growing up here amongst the brave Westlanders and the wonderment of Fairy Folk. I also look forward to meeting the other peoples that Queen Gemeenah has spoken about."

King Roland paused to hold Princess Iadore up once again.

"I present to all of you Princess Iadore Daisy!" King Roland stood, decked out in all of his royal regalia. He was every inch a King. In his Welcome Blessing speech he also expressed his desires to stay and his hopes that the Westlanders would feel the same way. Princess Iadore was laid in an ornately decorated bassinette on the platform. People formed a line to form a processional, giving each a moment to greet the baby and welcome her to the world. The fairies joined the line and followed suit.

When all of the greetings were finished the whole community sat to enjoy a glorious feast. Both Queen Gemeenah and King Roland watched their people, observed how the two races socialized together.

Before the meal was done, Queen Gemeenah leaned over to King Roland and whispered, "I am greatly pleased that you wish to stay. I know we initially agreed to rule our people individually. You rule your people and I rule mine, but I would like to suggest a co-ruler ship. I think we can rule both our peoples together."

"I agree." King Roland nodded.

Chapter Seven

"Thank you all for coming. Let us begin." King Roland looked around the room at the meeting. The King's council came to discuss the future of the Westlanders. Everyone around the table was already aware of the King's thoughts on the subject.

"I will give each of you a chance to have your say but first I would like to hear from our newest council member. Arlen, please tell me what the people have to say. What have you been hearing?" King Roland inquired.

Arlen was taken aback and humbled by the King's attention. He felt very uncomfortable in the spot light, but knew he had to somehow summon the courage to fulfill his duties to the King. After squirming for a moment, he cleared his throat gave his report.

"Ahem, well your majesty, the folks I have spoken to like it here. All but one man actually. The one man, Roman is his name, would like to continue the journey. He finds nothing wrong with living here. Well, I believe he just has a wandering bone in him." A look of pride came over Arlen's face. He had done well. He was pleased with himself. Maybe he belonged here after all.

King Roland nodded understandingly at Arlen and then questioned the rest of the council members. "And what does the rest of the council think?" The council members all agreed with Arlen's thoughts on the people wanting to stay, although only Arlen was familiar with Roman.

"Queen Gemeenah and I have decided that we would rule together. We would like for our peoples to come together as one community. I expressed my feelings as much at Princess Iadore's Welcome Blessing. I did so to lend some assurance to her. I sincerely want the Westlanders to feel as I do, but I do not dare to hope. Since we are going to stay, I would like committees formed to make our stay more permanent. We will need houses and stables. No more living in tents and such."

King Roland looked around seeing that the council members felt as he did about the tents. The tents served their purpose as temporary housing but actual walls and doors were missed.

"Arlen, can you ask Roman to come see me?" Arlen nodded but was not sure if that meant the meeting was over. "I am going to ask Queen Gemeenah to appoint some of her people to work with the committees. Working together as one kingdom is how we will create a harmonious community." With that, King Roland rose to leave and the council members rose as well. Arlen saw what was happening and jumped up so fast that he knocked his chair over, making a horribly loud bang. This caused everyone to jump in alarm.

King Roland walked over to Arlen and placed a hand on his shoulder.

"Arlen fear not. Be yourself. There is no right or wrong way to behave. I chose you for speaking out to address the concerns of your family and friends. You spoke freely and frankly then and I truly wish you to continue to do so. I have come to believe that sometimes the best way to handle royal issues is to go with non-royal actions. Be at peace, my friend. You are most welcome here. You have done well today and I appreciate you just as you are." Sincerity flowed from the King to Arlen's ears.

Arlen was slightly ashamed of himself for every time he had secretly harbored negative thoughts about the King. He is a solid, good man. He managed to stumbled over a "Yes, Your Majesty" as the King took his leave. He was not sure how the rest of the council members felt about him, but he felt that he was accepted by the king and hoped the members would eventually feel the same. Gratefully, he had no need to worry about the other members. They welcomed him to the group eagerly. With the meeting over, the council members all went their separate ways to begin working on the perspective committees. They were all curious about working with the fairy folk. King Roland headed out to go speak with Queen Gemeenah about the collaboration. The great venture that the Westlanders begun had changed, but only for the better.

Roman approached King Roland cautiously. He had never been the recipient of a royal summons before and worried that he had done something terribly wrong. He could not think of what he could have done. Nevertheless, he figured he just needed to clear up the issue. He was positive that whatever the King needed to see him for, it had to be some sort of misunderstanding.

"You wished to see me, Your Majesty?" Roman said loudly to both get the King's attention and to make sure he was heard.

King Roland turned around turned around to take measure of the man who had spoken. Seeing the questioning look on the King's face prodded Roman to explain further.

"My name is Roman. Arlen said you wanted to see me."

"Oh, yes! Good man!" King Roland had been lost in the conversation with a group of men he was standing with. He had completely forgotten his request to speak with Roman. "Please, come with me. I think we have much to discuss. Are you hungry? We can have a bite and talk." Turning towards the group of men, he said. "Please forgive me. I must take care of another matter that has come up. Shall we meet again tomorrow to finish?" Nods all around as King Roland took his leave.

"Yyyess, Your Majesty." Roman stammered while he followed the King. He still had no idea what the King about had to talk to him about. It seemed that life in the new kingdom was an ever evolving mystery.

Once the two men had settled in the royal tent, King Roland asked Sarah to bring them some refreshments. She curtsied in acknowledgement leaving the two men alone.

"Arlen tells me that you do not wish to stay here. You are free to go, of course. I would like to know if it is something here about the new Kingdom that you have an issue with or do you just have an adventurous spirit?" King Roland wasted no time in getting to the point of the meeting.

"Well, Your Majesty…."

"Please, stop with the King Roland's and the Your Majesty's. At this moment and for this meeting, I would prefer to just be two men having a casual conversation. Roland and Roman sharing food and stories. Is that all right with you?" King Roland interrupted.

"Well, all right then. If that is your wish, Yo… Roland." The words did not feel comfortable in Roman's mouth. "I do wish to leave but not because there is anything wrong here. Life here is actually really good. When I was a boy, I would dream of seeing what was on the other side of the Stolly Mountains. I never dared to even attempt to leave because of all of the stories I had heard all my life. No one returns. No one knew what was out there. What if there was nothing out there and I was left to die alone? Then, you proposed for us all to leave in the middle of the night. We abandoned everything we knew just with hope and a prayer that we would be able to find a new home. A place like this? Well, none of us could have imagined. And what about other kingdoms? Are they like ours? Do they have different kinds of government? What do they eat?" Roman paused to take a breath. "The journey sparked that old fire in me. I wanted to go further and see more. Finding the fairy kingdom was a complete shock. I mean who would have imagined that fairies were even real? And now, we find out that there are several magical peoples. We started out looking for a passage through the mountain to make a new home on the other side. Instead, we found a wonderful new home *inside* the mountain. Well, I still want to *see* the other side."

King Roland listened patiently and felt he understood completely. "When I was a boy I wanted to do so much, but from the time I could walk my father drilled me with the lessons of being a king. It did not matter if I wanted a different choice, I didn't by the way, but there was never even a choice for me. My brother was free to do as he wanted. And we know how that went. Awful! I often envied the boys in the kingdom. Choices seemed to abound for all of you. I was born to serve. I accepted and embraced that. It is all that I have ever known."

King Roland paused a moment, "When I proposed this journey, it was more of a quest for me to find a safe place for all of us, away from my brother. I had foolishly believed that we would find some land and restore the kingdom as it had been in my father's time. I see now that I did not consider that the new land might already have a kingdom. I see now that I was leaving one war to start another. We would be seen as an invading force. Finding the cavern and the fairy kingdom could not have been more fortuitous for us. I have known from the first day that Queen Gemeenah revealed her kingdom to us that she could have done away with all of us with a wave of her hand. We are lucky that she chose instead to get to know us. She and I have entered into an agreement to co-rule the cavern. Of course, we have not worked out all the details but I do not believe there will be any issues that cannot be resolved with discussion."

King Roland paused to see if Roman was still listening. He was unaware that he was rambling a bit. "I am sorry. I guess I have a lot of things swirling about in my head. Thank you for listening and letting me get this out. However, this is not the reason I asked to speak with you. What I wanted to ask is, are you planning on returning?"

Roman sat thoughtful for a moment. He was considering all that King Roland had shared and was pondering the question posed.

"Honestly, I had not thought that far ahead." Roman admitted with a chuckle. "I just simply want to see more. I suppose that at some point, yes I will be coming back. I do have family and friends that I will miss. I just cannot provide any kind of time."

"Of course, now you say family. Are you married? Do you have children?" King Roland wanted to know who Roman would be leaving behind and what needed to be done to care for them in his absence.

"Oh, no! I meant my mother and father. I have a brother as well. My sister is married with a family of her own." Roman quickly answered. The questions somehow made him feel as if his character as a man was being questioned.

"I meant no offense in my questions. I just wanted to know so that I can be sure that any family left behind would be provided for. You see, I am in the mind of making you the very first royal ambassador of our kingdom. I suppose that we will need to determine the name of our new kingdom first, but my thought is that I would like it if you would agree to be a royal ambassador. The new places that you go will treat you with more respect as an ambassador than as just a wanderer. You could meet with the rulers in peace. You would have authority to offer trade, if it is even possible. I do not know yet what we will have to trade, but it is still a good way to start. I also hope that an ambassadorship would offer you some degree of protection during your travels. What do you think?" King Roland expressed all of his ideas and concerns in a rush.

Roman was moved by the earnestness of the king's words.

"Plus, I want to know what you discover. My curiosity is as great as yours. I do not, however, have the nerve or the freedom." King Roland added.

Roman smiled. "I do not believe it is a question of your nerve, Roland. You have, and have always had, great responsibilities. You confessed to being envious of us common folk but I was envious of you as well. I had to clean up after the animals, tend the garden, all kinds of stuff. I constantly had work to do. I thought that you had it easy. I have come to believe, to know, differently. I have watched you. I noticed that you travelled up and down the line checking on and doing all that you could for each of us. You did that every day. You were genuinely concerned for each of us. I did not envy you then that's for sure. I am an ordinary man. Just plain and common. A simple man. I do not want to embarrass you or our kingdom by my lack of knowledge or manners."

"Well, that is the beauty of it. How could you embarrass me? One, they will have no idea who "we" are or how "we" behave. If you do anything that is offensive to the people you meet, just apologize explain that it is how "we" do whatever it was here. It is not like they would know or even be able to find out." King Roland was so amused with himself for thinking of this. He could not hide it.

Roman considered this and replied, "Well, I guess that could work. What would be involved with the ambassador thing?"

"Nothing really is required. I just thought that I could have my counselors write a document explaining who you are and that you are an ambassador to our Kingdom. It will say that you are traveling to see new communities and to discover any possible peace treaties that can be formed and to establish trade. My hope is that you will be treated with some respect and no harm will come to you." King Roland continued, "I admit that I am looking forward to your tales of adventure. If you would not mind, take notes and be descriptive. This way, it will be as though I were with you. May be even experience some of the excitement that you felt as it happened."

"Well, I guess the only thing left to settle on is the name of the kingdom that I am from." Roman stated this as a way of accepting the King's offer.

"I believe that is my cue to have a meeting with Queen Gemeenah. I will have the counselors draft the documents that you will need and provide you with a few books of blank paper for your notes. Thank you for accepting my offer." King Roland and Roman left the tent. Each began their preparations. Each excited for the future.

The cavern was divided up into homesteads. Each family was to get a small house with a bit of land for gardening. The fairies lived in crevices along the cavern walls. This left the floor of the cavern available for the humans. The houses were simple and with the fairies help, quickly built. The fairies included items in the houses that were new to the humans. For example, the humans normally got buckets of water from the stream to use for cooking and cleaning. The fairies put water vines. The humans were in awe of such conveniences. No more buckets!

King Roland insisted that everyone else get their homes established before his own. As always, he put his people and their needs first. When the last homestead was settled, the council presented King Roland with the plan design for his castle. King Roland resoundingly rejected the idea.

"I am honored and flattered but I have no need of a castle. There is no threat of war or my brother to contend with. I require a modest home for Princess Iadore and myself. I would like room for Sarah and Susan. They have been helping me care for Princess Iadore and I would like to make a place for them in my home. Perhaps the only thing I would like differently is a dining room large enough to hold council meetings. I do not see a need for a separate room. Yes. I believe that would work nicely." King Roland stated loudly enough for all to hear. "If I wish to be truly honest, I never felt very comfortable at the castle in Circlandia. I grew up there but there was more space than people. I used to get lost in there as a child. There was nothing cozy or warm about it. I never knew true comfort until I married Queen Isadora. She is what made the castle a home to me and many times I had to go search for her. Imagine that. Losing your wife in your home! It was awful. I do not want this for Princess Iadore."

"Of course, your Majesty. We will start over at once. I was unaware that you felt this way. You are ever an amazement to me." said Maxwell. As the councilman in charge of housing, he was responsible for the home designs and the image of the kingdom. A kingdom with no castle is a new challenge that he welcomed. A home for the modest, unassuming King of Westfairland.

Chapter Eight

Years went by. Life in the cavern was turning out to be all that was hoped for. The humans and the fairies worked together in harmony. Each had taught the other much. Queen Gemeenah and King Roland divided up the ruling by race but often consulted one another when advice was needed. Ambassador Roman came home about once a year. There was always a celebration when he returned. The people of Westfairland would gather in the center of the village to hang on Roman's every word. The stories of his adventures were captivating. Roman found as much joy in being a story teller as he did as a traveler.

Through Roman's journeys, trade was indeed established. The Westfairlanders traded their vegetables and cheeses for fabrics and laces. Roman would also have private meetings with Queen Gemeenah and King Roland to go over his journals. He made every effort to capture what he experienced as it was happening. He soon understood King Roland's desire to feel as he did when coming across new things. Roman told them about the various types of government that he encountered. There was one country that had a president. A president was voted into office by the people.

Another kingdom that was ruled by a Queen chosen through a pageant. All of the young ladies from the age of fifteen summers on would be in a contest to determine which was the most beautiful, most talented, and most intelligent. Once a Queen was found, she would hold a tournament for all the eligible young men. The Queen would set a series of challenges and quests for the men to compete. This would continue until only one man was left. In this way, a King was found. The King and Queen rule together. The people believe that in this way they have the best possible woman and the best possible man as leaders for the best possible country.

Just like in the village square, Queen Gemeenah and King Roland were a rapt audience. They marveled at how differently people lived. Roman would also bring back strange fruit and sometimes an animal. He also brought back some money and explained how it was used to buy merchandise. This was a hard concept for the royals to understand. There was no currency in Westfairland and yet everyone had all their needs met. The purpose of money was lost on them.

Princess Iadore was six years old now. She knew that these were private meetings but she would always hide to listen any way. She was ever curious and the delight of all. During the day, she had lessons with her two teachers, one human and one fairy. She was taught the ways of both races and how they lived in harmony. She tried to be good all the time and seldom caused any problems. When she did get into trouble, it was due to her inability to control her adventurous nature.

Roman was her favorite person in her world. She could listen to his stories for hours on end. Her governess, Sarah, would often scold her and implored her to keep her feet on solid ground. As soon as Roman left Princess Iadore would begin her own adventures. She would climb the cavern walls and pretend to be looking for new kingdoms. She would crawl through garden imagining the wild animals she would encounter in the jungles. Her imagination was limitless. She basically pretended to be Roman. As a result, Princess Iadore was becoming almost impossible to keep track of.

One fateful day, she climbed particularly high. She intentionally chose a dark corner of the cavern. She had hopes that no one would discover her, giving her time to reach new heights. And she did. Suddenly, she lost her grip and plunged to the cavern floor. A spike of jagged rock ripped through her back, piercing her heart. Sadly, just as the Princess had wanted, no one saw her. More importantly, no one saw her fall. In fact, at this particular moment, no one was even looking for her. Sarah was preparing Princess Iadore's lunch. The search for her began while her lunch went cold.

Once the search had begun, more and more villagers joined in. Where could she have gone? She had to be here somewhere. It was a cavern, after all, with only so much space. She had to be here. King Roland had said these words many times during the search, almost as if he were trying to make the words true just by repeating them. There would be consequences this time. He felt awful about all the concern that Princess Iadore's antics were causing. The time for firm rules had come.

All of these thoughts and feelings melted away when King Roland first spotted Princess Iadore lying motionless on the cavern floor. She was so still. Fear gripped his heart. For a moment, he was unmoving in place. Then he rushed to Princess Iadore's side, but he was afraid to touch her. He knew her wound was serious.

Queen Gemeenah saw the crowd and came down to see what was happening. She too was frightened by the site of the Princess and her grievous injury. Gracefully, she pushed Sarah and King Roland away from the Princess. Sweet, tender tears escaped her eyes. She knew that the Princess would not live unless she acted.

Queen Gemeenah pulled a thorn dagger from her belt. As gently as she could she cut through Princess Iadore's dress and her chest where her heart was failed to beat. She picked up the princess to lay her flat on the ground. Then without any warning, Queen Gemeenah sliced open her own chest. She reached inside her chest pulling out a handful of her fairy light. She placed the fairy light into Princess Iadore's wound. Her heart glowed and slowly began to beat. Queen Gemeenah then cut her finger using her healing blood to close both of their wounds. Violet had appeared behind Queen Gemeenah holding the enchanted daisy blanket.

After a few moments of thick silence, Princess Iadore gasped a deep breath. Her eyelids fluttered open. Queen Gemeenah said to no one in particular that the Princess would need rest, but she would be all right now. Then, she looked at King Roland and said, "She is as much my child as she is yours now."

King Roland did not quite understand what Queen Gemeenah had done. He sensed the truth of her words. He had seen the healed wounds. He thought to himself that a talk with Queen Gemeenah was coming, but for now, his primary worry was Princess Iadore.

King Roland carried Princess Iadore home. Sarah continually muttering apologies, followed behind. Halfway there, King Roland stopped to assure her that he knew his daughter and knew that she was not to blame. Once home King Roland laid Princess Iadore down to rest. Sarah brought her the lunch she had prepared earlier. King Roland instructed her not to warm up her lunch. Cold lunch is the least of the punishments the princess would endure. In truth, he already knew how frazzled Sarah was and did not want her to be troubled more.

After lunch, King Roland admonished Princess Iadore and told her that she was to remain in bed to rest. She was in fact not to leave her room! He wanted to hear no complaints or excuses. Princess Iadore had never seen her father so angry. She knew better than to question or disobey this time.

Queen Gemeenah was lying on her pink rose petal bed. She too was resting to recover from her sacrifice to save the Princess. Violet brought her some wildflower nectar and fruit on a tray.

"Why did you do it?" Violet asked.

"Do you remember when Queen Isadora passed away? How sad King Roland was? When I first met the King, I learned his heart. I knew his intentions were good and I wanted to make sure that his people felt the same. I wanted to make sure that there was not a dissident among the group that would cause trouble. I cast a spell on King Roland and all the Westlanders while they slept. King Roland's thoughts and feelings would be tied to his people. If he was happy and wanting a harmonious kingdom, then his people would be happy and want a harmonious kingdom. At the time, I could not have imagined the loss of Queen Isadora." Queen Gemeenah sighed. "I knew then that the spell had worked. All of his people were gripped by the same grief and depression. That is why I was so determined to help him through his loss so that he could focus on the Princess."

Queen Gemeenah paused to take a moment to reflect on her decisions.

"I also could not have imagined how fond I would become of the humans. I truly do love Princess Iadore. Her father named her correctly. I adore her. I gave half my fairy light to heal her heart and save the Westlanders from the deep despair of their king with the loss of his only child. I do not believe that King Roland would be able to survive the loss of her. Neither could I for that matter. Now we are all truly connected."

Chapter Nine

Two years went by. Princess Iadore had developed fairy gifts after Queen Gemeenah healed her heart. She could now understand animal thoughts. This came in handy when any of the farm animals became sick or injured. She could not make flowers grow from a seed but she could make buds bloom and she could make blooms bigger. She was a true representative of both races.

Peace flowed through Westfairland. Princess Iadore no longer had to be told to keep off the cavern walls. She still had an adventurous spirit but no longer had the desire to climb. All her daydreams now showed her staying firmly on the ground.

Roman started to make his annual trips home during the festival week. His story telling became a part of the celebration. No one wanted to miss the chance to listen to his tales. Princess Iadore secretly harbored a desire to go with Roman one day when she was old enough, but the memory of her fall was never far from her mind. She often touched her scar to remind herself to stay on the ground and to stay safe in the cavern.

This year, the Westfairland festival was exceptional. A processional from King Minegard's dwarf clan came to join in the celebration. The humans had known about the existence of dwarves for years, but this is the first time meeting them. Princess Iadore still wore the daisy crown the dwarves made for her. The crown had been enchanted to grow as the princess grew. This ensured that the crown would always be a perfect fit. Roman's adventures had now become the stuff of legend. King Minegard looked forward to hearing the stories for himself first hand.

Princess Iadore completely charmed King Minegard. He had learned about her accident and knew that she was now a half fairy. She was enthralled by him as well. They talked for hours in what seemed like minutes. The Dwarves brought many treasures to Westfairland. Nectar flowed in all the cups. Every dish of food was devoured. Everyone agreed this was the most joyous festival yet.

After the festival, Princess Iadore had become wistful for the daring exploits of Roman once again. This feeling only grew stronger after meeting King Minegard and the dwarves. The desire was so strong that she could no longer deny herself a little exploration. Roman and the fairies were the only ones that knew how to navigate the cave tunnels to get to the outside world. This information was kept secret to protect Westfairland. Princess Iadore thought she could go into the cave tunnel just a little way and then return before anyone was the wiser.

The cave tunnel was terribly dark. A torch barely made enough light for the princess to see. The tunnel immediately turned and split into four new tunnels. I should turn back now she thought, but then decided she would go just a little farther down the tunnel on the right before turning back. Her curiosity got the better of her once again. She continued without paying attention to where she had come from, turning down tunnel after tunnel. There were so many choices! The farther she got from Westfairland, the darker the tunnels became. There was no longer fairy light to guide her. Her torch had burned out.

Soon she found herself in complete darkness and very, very scared. It was time to turn back! But she could not find her way home. Dragging her hand along the wall she walked on. She had walked for what seemed like hours in the darkness. Tears could no longer be held back. She knew that she had made a grave mistake and began to fear that she would never see her home again.

Sarah realized that she could not find Princess Iadore anywhere. She had looked and looked. She did not want to raise the alarm just yet. After two hours of looking, she finally had to alert King Roland. Once again everyone in the kingdom was searching for the Princess. Every one trying not to think about what happened the last time the princess had gone missing. Arlen found her footprints leading into the cave tunnels.

Queen Gemeenah came over to see for herself. She confirmed that those were the Princess' footsteps. King Roland immediately ordered the villagers to search the tunnels. Queen Gemeenah stopped the search before it began. She explained that it would be safer for the fairies to conduct the search. The tunnels were very dark and people would get lost. The fairy folk had their light and could see in the darkness.

She also reassured him that no harm had come to the Princess. She was just lost. Since they shared fairy light, Queen Gemeenah would know if Princess Iadore was hurt. She would feel any pain the Princess would experience. King Roland took small comfort in this knowledge, but agreed to let the fairies conduct the search for his daughter.

A few days of searching had gone by with no sign of the Princess. King Roland sat on his modest throne in the meeting room of his house. Each day, he moved less and less. Each day, he ate less and less. All of the Westlanders did the same. Queen Gemeenah became worried about the lives of the humans. So she cast another spell immobilizing them all until the Princess returned. This way, none would suffer from hunger or even age. Once the Princess came home, the humans would be restored as they were. None the wiser.

The fairies continued the search. Days of searching spread into weeks and slowly faded into months. Then, the months became years. There was no sign of the Princess. The cave tunnels were endless. There was no telling how long it would take to find her. All the fairies deeply missed their human friends. None were willing to give up the hope of bringing the Princess home and restoring their kingdom.

What the peoples of Westfairland did not know is that Princess Iadore had walked for so long in the dark that when she finally saw light again, she broke into a run. She had no way of knowing that she had been walking in the darkness for eleven days!

"Home!" she yelled. "I will never leave again. I just want to hug my father. I hope he will forgive me." She made many promises to herself during her ordeal. But regretfully, she was not home. She had burst out of the cave and noticed that the gemlight was very different. There were no colors to be seen. Just white. Everything was white and mushy. That's odd she thought. Then she saw the moon.

It was a cold, cold night with a halfmoon in a spray of stars above.

Princess Iadore did not know what to do. She knew that she had made it out of the caves and knew that she did not find her way home. She didn't know where she was or what she was seeing. She also knew she would never see her true home again. She walked for a bit on the soft mushy white ground. Her only hope was to find someone, anyone that would help her. When no one came, she lay down in the cold and cried herself to sleep.

There a kind hunter found her. He carried her to his home to care for her. Since Princess Iadore could not tell the kind hunter how to find Westfairland, he raised her as his own. He called her Dorie and did all that he could to make her happy. He was captivated by her special gifts though he did not believe that she was half fairy. She lived out her days as the daughter of the kind hunter. She eventually married and had children of her own. All things considered, Princess Iadore had a good life as Dorie Hunter.

Her life in Westfairland became stories of whimsy. Some would even call her stories fairytales.

Many, many years had passed.

Queen Gemeenah clutched her heart with a gasp. She collapsed on her pink rose petal bed.

"What is it, my Queen?" Violet asked as she rushed to her side.

"Princess Iadore is gone from this world. Her light did not return to me. She must have had a child to pass my light on to." Queen Gemeenah sobbed.

"Should I tell everyone to stop searching for her?

"No." Queen Gemeenah sighed. "I do not want all hope to be lost. There has to be a way to revive our human friends."

Part Two

Presently

Chapter Ten

"Hello there. Aren't you a handsome bunny?" asked Ilove. "It's a beautiful day out and about in the woods today."

"The grass is sweet in the shade." replied Mr. Bunny, twitching his cotton ball tail ever so slightly.

"Naturally. There's some wild clover over there." She points out.

Mr. Bunny raises his head to see where Ilove is indicating. "Mmm. Good eye! That looks delicious." Off he hops to feast on the bright green clover.

Looking around, Ilove spots the Robins and congratulates them on their hatchlings.

"I look forward to seeing your little ones fly someday, Mrs. Robin."

"It won't be long. They grow so fast!" says Mrs. Robin.

Ilove has many animal friends. She reads them stories and they tell her about their life in the woods at the edge of town. Almost daily, as soon as she is free from school, Ilove flees to the woods to play. Today, of course, was no different. Until she realized she was hearing some new voices in the woods. Curious as always, she went to look for the source.

"What new friends would I make today?" she wondered.

Out of the corner of her eye, she spotted two dragonflies by the meandering creek, one brilliant blue and one vibrant green. Their colors so bright, they almost seemed to glow a bit.

"Aren't these wildflowers the dreamiest, Clover?" asked Azure as she flew through the white petals. Yellow pollen dappled her body and wings.

"It's Cloven! How many times do I have to tell you?" Clover sniped. "Clover just does not fit who I am!"

"You're a green fairy! Your name is Clover! It's time to embrace it!" Azure replied gleefully for having this conversation again for the millionth time.

"Hello." Ilove interrupted their conversation. Azure was so startled that she crashed into a dandelion that cushioned her landing. The dandelion burst, sending its seedlings away with the wind.

"Just pretend you meant to do that, Az. It's a human. She is probably just saying hello like all the dumb humans do. I don't know why they talk to animals when they cannot actually understand animals or us for that matter." Clover cautioned.

"Not true. I mean you are right about most humans, but I understand you perfectly. My name is Ilove."

Both dragonflies stared, tiny mouths gaping, neither dared to move a muscle. Well, this is a first.

"She acts like she can hear us. She's very convincing. I'll give her that." Azure said, giving into a little shake to knock off some of the pollen.

"I can hear you truly. I know it's not common. My mother says that I mustn't tell anyone that I can understand animals and talk to them. She says that people will think I'm full of non-sense. Honestly, I think she doesn't really believe me. I'm guessing it's not a very common thing." Ilove explained.

"Hmm. She's very convincing." Clover whispered.

"I'm convincing because I can hear you. Do you have names? And why did you call her a green fairy? She is clearly a dragonfly."

"Whaaaatt....?" Azure uttered. "Did I say that? You must have misunderstood. She is a dragonfly all right."

"Oh, stop being silly. I know what I heard. Are dragonflies similar to fairies? We, humans I mean, have lots of stories about fairies, but everyone says they are not real. So, are you the same and maybe long ago there was a person like me that told everyone else fairies are real? That would explain where the stories came from. Wouldn't you think? I mean just think about it! Fairies being real! And dragonflies! And dragonflies are everywhere! Does this mean that fairies are everywhere?" Ilove was rambling with excitement. "Oh, this is wonderful!"

Azure and Clover were stunned. They both understood at the same time that Ilove really could understand them. The discovery of fairies by humans was forbidden. All magical creatures knew that humans were dangerous. Not knowing what else to do, the fairies looked at each other and flew away immediately.

"I'm sorry! I didn't mean to scare you! Please come back!" Ilove called after them, disappointment dripping from every syllable. "Oh drat! I ruined it with my prattling! Fairies are real! Who knew such a thing could be true. I thought that was just a fairytale!" She scolded herself repeatedly as she walked home.

Chapter Eleven

"We must tell the Queen!" Azure yelled.

"No! We will get in trouble for slipping out again. You remember last time she threatened to clip our wings!" Clover shouted back.

"She will know any way. She always does. Better to just come out with it. A human that can talk to animals! More importantly, a human that knows about us! Who knew such a thing could be true! I thought that was just a human tale!" Azure marveled.

The fairies were well within the cave tunnels leading to Westfairland and the cavern village they call home. Azure and Clover would often sneak out to explore the human world. Their home was full of humans that were under an Unmoving Enchantment. The fairies tended to the humans by keeping them dusted. Constantly, they searched for signs of life or any indication that the enchantment was breaking.

The legend states that Queen Gemeenah opened the cavern up to welcome the humans. They, fairies and humans, lived together peacefully and in complete harmony until the human king lost his only beloved daughter. She got lost in the cave tunnels and was never seen again. Queen Gemeenah believed that once the girl was found that life in Westfairland would go back to the way it was so she cast the enchantment hoping to save the humans from the sadness and pain the loss of the Princess caused. She still thinks the Princess will come back one day, but it's been many, many years.

Azure and Clover never knew the humans when they were awake. They were born after all of this occurred. Edward is the only human that they know but he does not count. Woody brought him to the cavern one day many years ago. Violet saved him with her fairy light. Any time a human is saved by fairy light, the human becomes a half fairy. So does he even really count? Azure and Clover did not think so.

"Where have you been?" Queen Gemeenah yelled at Azure and Clover the second they burst into the cavern. They had wisely changed back into their fairy forms half way through the tunnels.

"We were searching the tunnels for the girl, Your Majesty." Clover said a touch too quickly.

"Really? Then why do you smell of sunshine? Did you leave the tunnels to go outside into the human world? Were you seen?" Queen Gemeenah always knew what the young ones were up to. They were born about fifty years after Princess Iadore went missing. The fairies were missing the humans and the joy that Princess Iadore brought to everyday life with her childish ways and insatiable curiosity. Two fairy couples decided it was time to bring new life into the cavern. Fairy folk have very long life spans. They take the decision of bringing new life into the world very seriously. Azure and Clover were the then born.

"We were seen by a human girl. We were disguised as dragonflies." Azure confessed.

"Who taught you that trick?" Queen Gemeenah questioned.

"No one. We read about it in the scrolls. We thought it would be a good thing to know how to do in case we run into any humans in the tunnels while searching for the girl." Clover stated this a little too confidently.

"Really? And here I thought you learned this spell to go out into the forbidden human world and go unnoticed. Silly me!" Queen Gemeenah knew she was right by their embarrassed faces. "Did the human girl notice anything different about you two?

"Yes!" Azure blurted out.

"No!" Clover yelled.

Both at the same time.

"Explain." The queen demanded.

Clover was shooting daggers at Azure as if saying "Don't you dare!"

"It wasn't us, your majesty. I mean it was us, but she is the odd one. She thinks we are dragonflies." Azure shied away from Clover to answer the queen. "She, the girl I mean, could understand us. She can talk to animals."

Queen Gemeenah looked at Clover for confirmation of what Azure had said. Clover, afraid to make eye contact with the Queen, just simply nodded.

"There is more. She overheard me call Clover a green fairy. She asked a ton of questions that we did not answer. Then she rambled on for a bit. We were too stunned to say anything more. We left her believing that fairies and dragonflies were the same thing. We did not know what else to do. We, I am, most sorry, Your Majesty." Azure blushed with shame.

"It is "we", Your Majesty. I am also very sorry. I was once again attempting to get Azure to call me Cloven. I have yet to understand why no one will grant me this one small request." Clover added.

"Quite simply, it is because your given name is Clover, dear. Acceptance of who you are will bring you peace." Queen Gemeenah replied casually. Clover attempted to explain and stopped before she could utter so much as a word. "Do not bother. I know you do not feel like a "Clover". I have heard your explanation. A name is not who you are. A name is a name. Embrace who you are. You are a green fairy. Clover is your name. You can call yourself Cloven or Mushroom and you will still be green and you will still be a fairy."

Queen Gemeenah placed a gentle understanding hand on Clover's shoulder. "I know you are having a hard time finding your place here. You will find your place and your own unique way to stand out. You will own your embrace identity. But a name change will not do the trick." Turning to Azure, "You must take me to this girl immediately!"

"We cannot, your majesty. It is dark time there. We met her in the woods by the creek. I am sure she will be at home for sleep. We can take you tomorrow. I think she spends a lot of time in the woods. The girl seems very comfortable there."

"Yes, of course. Tomorrow then, but tell no one else of this. Not even your parents. That is a command!" Queen Gemeenah left to go to her chamber, eager for the morning. She was also afraid to hope. Could this girl be a descendant of Iadore? Has her half-light been found after all these years? Would the enchantment finally be broken? Her mind was racing. Could it really be? After all this time?

Chapter Twelve

Ilove raced down to the creek after school. She hoped against hope that the dragonflies would be back so she could apologize for her behavior. She didn't mean to be rude. She thought that if she said she was sorry and asked if they could start again, they were sure to be friends.

She found the dragonflies down by the creek, just like the day before. Today, however, there were three. The new dragonfly was unlike any she had seen before. This one appeared to be somewhat white with lots of muted colors running through.

"Wow!" Ilove exclaimed. "You are so beautiful. You look like an opal pendant that my mother has. Hers is just an oval stone, not a dragonfly, of course. Hello Azure and Clover! Good to see you again today. I wanted to tell you that I am most sorry for how I acted yesterday. Can we please start over? I would love for us to be friends."

"You were not rude. We were just caught off guard yesterday. We have never known a human that could speak dragonfly." Azure said.

"What about fairy? Do humans and fairies speak the same language?" Ilove asked.

"No… no… I told you. That was a misunderstanding. We are clearly dragonflies." Azure persisted.

"Pish posh! How are we to be friends if we cannot be honest with each other? I know you called Clover a green fairy. You told her she needed to embrace that fact. You didn't say dragonfly. You said fairy!" Ilove knew what she heard and she wasn't about to back down.

Queen Gemeenah gasped. "So it is true. You can understand us. Can you talk to all animals?"

"Why yes I can. I used to think that everyone could, but I have learned that I seem to be the only one. My mother says that I shouldn't tell people that I can talk to animals. They will think I've gone a little off in the head. My name is Ilove. May I ask your name?"

"My name is Queen Gemeenah. You use words that I've never heard before but I can get the gist of what you are saying."

"Oh my! A queen! Dragonfly queen or fairy queen?" Ilove asked slyly.

"Great question." Queen Gemeenah replied dismissively. "Who is your mother? Do you know Iadore?"

Ilove noticed the Queen acknowledge and then dodge her question. Tricksy.

"My mother's name is Trailynn Kingston. My father was Richard Kingston. He promised when he left for the war that he would come back, but mommy says that he won't be coming home. So it's just me and my mom. We live in a little cottage at the edge of the woods. Just outside of town. Where do you live?" Ilove hoped that if she just kept sneaking in little questions here and there, some might get answered. "Also, I don't know any one named Iadore. Is she a friend of yours?

"Richard? War? Interesting." Surely it can't be the same war that caused Roland and his people to flee. That has to just be a coincidence. Plus, they came from the other side of the mountain. That passage has never been reopened. And she's never heard of Iadore. So much to learn about this child. "Talking to animals is not usually a human trait. Can you do anything else?"

"I don't think so, but my mother says that I have a green thumb."

There was no coloring on any of her fingers or anywhere else that she could see.

"Why would she say that? None of your fingers or thumbs are green. You are human colored only?" Queen Gemeenah was clearly confused by the comment.

Ilove giggled. "No, she doesn't mean that I literally have a green thumb. She means that the vegetables and other plants seem to grow for me better than they do for her. We have a small garden. Six rows. That means that we each have to tend to three rows. My rows just seem to grow bigger and produce more than my mothers. I think it because I sing while I work. My mother tried that too but I think the plants just like my voice better."

"Ah… I see." Queen Gemeenah felt her fairy light pulse a bit when she first met Ilove. She has Iadore's fairy gifts. She feels quite certain that Ilove is a descendant of Iadore's. Could she possibly wake up her friends and restore Westfairland? How can she find out and still keep the magical creatures' secrecy pact?

"I know you have many questions, but I am unable to answer them at the moment. There are many issues to be considered. Do you come here often?"

"I'm here almost every day. I love the woods. I feel more at home here than in my actual home." Ilove confessed. "I've never told my mother that. I'm afraid it would hurt her feelings. We have a nice home. It's just that here, I feel like I can breathe and be myself more."

"Good. I mean, good that you will be around here. Well, and good that you have a nice home. Also, I think I understand about the other bit. I would very much like to get to know you better. I will visit again in a day or so. I have others that I must speak with before we spend too much time together." Queen Gemeenah took off. Azure and Clover waited a minute.

"Azure and Cloven, I hope to see you again as well."

"You called me Cloven?" Clover said completely elated.

"Of course. I know your name is Clover, but if you prefer Cloven. It's the least I can do." Ilove replied with a smile. "I truly hope we can be friends."

"Me too. See you in a day or so." Clover and Azure left to rejoin the Queen.

Chapter Thirteen

Four very long days later, the dragonflies had returned much to Ilove's delight!

"There you are! I was afraid you would never return!" Ilove exclaimed.

"I apologize for the long wait. There were many things that I had to consider. Many others that I had to consult. I have much I to tell you and I am not sure exactly how to go about it." Queen Gemeenah explained. "I do not wish to overwhelm you or frighten you."

"Well, I do not have any fear of you. Why don't you just go ahead and tell me whatever it is. If I start to freak out, I'll let you know." Ilove offered.

"I am not sure what "freak out" means but I will assume it means that you will become afraid? All right then." Queen Gemeenah gave a little nod to Azure and Clover. "This might be a bit of a shock."

The three dragonflies started to glow brighter. They became balls of light that continued to grow in size. In one last burst of color, the fairies stood before Ilove in their true form. No one spoke. Ilove stared in disbelief at first. Slowly, Ilove shook her head a bit. As if she were trying to clear her head or perhaps make the illusion go away.

"You did overhear Azure correctly. We are fairy folk. Please sit. I have a story to tell you. In the end, you will understand how the story relates to you." Queen Gemeenah paused, and then added "I hope."

Ilove found a soft grassy spot to make herself comfortable. "This should be interesting." she thought to herself.

"Oh, interesting indeed." Queen Gemeenah said with a wink. "We also brought some refreshments to help pass the time." Azure produced some large flowers that Clover poured some wildflower nectar into. "Normally, we drink fresh spring water, but on special occasions we enjoy wildflower nectar. These are butter cookies. We have some human friends that introduced us to these many years ago. I do not think ours are quite as good as the ones our friends made, but they are not bad."

Holding a flower cup in one hand, Ilove numbly helped herself to one of the offered cookies. She gave it a quick sniff before taking a tentative nibble. The cookie seemed to melt in her mouth. Her taste buds exploded with a warm butter taste with a hint of some kind of berry. She wasn't sure.

"Oh my! This is the most yummiest cookie I've ever had! I would very much like to try your friends' cookies if you think that they are even better!" Then she took a small sip of the wildflower nectar. "Wow! That is delicious. Please take your time telling your story. I don't mind spending an afternoon with fairies sharing these kinds of treats!" Ilove cried out with a giggle. "Did I really just say that?" She thought. Looking around, Ilove spotted Mr. Bunny and a few of her other animal friends. "Do you mind if I invite my friends to join us?"

"Of course not." Queen Gemeenah said.

Mr. Bunny, Mrs. Robin, and several other animals gathered around to settle around Ilove. "Are we all ready? Let me begin. Long, long ago..."

Queen Gemeenah began her story to the time right before King Roland and the Westlanders came to the cavern and stopped when Iadore was lost. Ilove listened attentively eating cookies and drinking nectar. The fairies let her be. Realizing she was considering all that she had been told.

Slowly, Ilove nodded her head.

"If I understand the story, you shared your light to heal the princess, cast the Unmoving Enchantment after Princess Iadore's disappearance, and the search continues. But what does this have to do with me?" Ilove eventually asked.

"Funny you should ask. I know that Iadore is no longer alive. Humans do not live as long as fairies, not even half humans. When Iadore left this world, the light that I gave her should have returned, making my fairy light whole. That did not happen which means that Iadore had at least one child. She passed her fairy light onto her child. The light would continue to be passed down mother to child. Iadore had a few fairy abilities after I healed her heart. She could make plants, garden items you see, grow larger and she could converse with animals. Sound familiar?" Queen Gemeenah explained.

Ilove gasped. "You mean that you think that I am Iadore's descendant?"

"Yes. That is exactly what I mean. If I am right, you may be the only person capable of breaking the Unmoving Enchantment and freeing our friends."

Ilove jumped to her feet. "What do I need to do? I'm not saying I believe you, but I'll do what I can to help. Plus, I have to at least give your story the benefit of doubt. I mean you are fairies and you are here. Like really here. So… well there is that. So…well…if this much is true. I have to at least try."

Chapter Fourteen

"Where have you been? I've been calling for you?" Trailynn shouted at Ilove. "I've been worried sick!"

"I'm sorry mommy! I was in the woods with the fairies. They told me the most amazing story!" Ilove excitedly explained. "I lost track of time and I didn't hear you at all."

"I've had enough with your stories, Ilove! Where were you?" Her mother demanded.

"I told you! I'm not lying. I was in the woods with the fairies." Ilove had never seen her mother so angry. She didn't understand how she could be mad since Ilove was telling the truth. "I'm sorry if I frightened you, but I really didn't hear you. It's just now turning dark. I know I have to be home before dark. Why are you so mad?"

"I'm angry because I called you in for dinner and couldn't find you!" Trailynn was exasperated with Ilove. "You know. I think it's time for you to get your head out of the clouds a bit. I love your wild imagination and the stories you come up with, but when I call for you, you need to answer. I think you should stay home for a while. No more going to the woods after school until I give you permission! Eat your cold dinner and go to your room." Trailynn turned her back on Ilove while she ate. She didn't know how to explain her tears. She didn't know if her tears were of relief or anger. How could she explain if she didn't quite understand herself? What if she had lost Ilove like the old tenant of this house had all those years ago?

"But mommy I can't! I'm supposed to go with the fairies to Westfairland on Saturday to see if I can free the people there from the Unmoving Enhancement!" Ilove cried out.

"ENOUGH!!!" her mother roared. "I don't want to hear any more fantasy stories right now! There is a time and a place for that. This isn't it! Eat and go to your room. NOW! Maybe tomorrow after you have had some time to think, you will face reality and tell me the truth. I believe you were in the woods playing. I believe you lost track of time. That's it. Just admit to that. There is no reason to add fairies to the story. Fairies are not real! And while I'm at it, animals don't talk. You are growing up Ilove. You need to start acting like it."

Ilove went to explain again that every word was true, but the look on her mother's face advised against it.

"Not another word." Trailynn said so sternly that Ilove instantly, and wisely, clamped her mouth shut.

Ilove finished her dinner and went to her room. There she cried and wondered what she could do. Tails, a small mouse that lived in her closet, came out to see what the matter was.

"What's the trouble child?" Tails inquired.

Ilove told Tails everything that had happened today. Tails was surprised, but didn't doubt a word. All animals knew about the magical races.

"You mustn't blame your mother. She loves you. After losing your father, she is terrified of losing you as well. And humans cannot normally talk to animals. I've always wondered why you could. Even if you are not Iadore's descendant, you are clearly very special." Tails offered as a way to soothe Ilove's emotions. "What shall we do?"

"We? You mean you will help me?" Ilove gratefully asked.

"Why wouldn't I? Who always sneaks me a bit of the best cheese?" Tails smiled. "You would be my friend even without the cheese thing. I am glad to help. I just don't know what I can do. It isn't like I can explain things to your mother."

"No I wouldn't think you could." Ilove smiled back. "Could you go to the woods on Saturday and let the fairies know what happened with my mother? Please tell them that I will still go with them the first Saturday that I can."

"Leave the house?" Just the thought of going back out into the woods terrified Tails. She still had bad dreams about being chased by cats and hiding from owls.

"Tell everyone that you're helping me. I'm sure that they will leave you alone. Tell them it's a secret mission." Ilove tried to be reassuring. She really couldn't promise that she would be left alone. "It's the only idea that I have. I just really do not want to disappoint the fairies. I really do want to help them if I can."

"Where do I have to go?" Tails asked. She couldn't hide her fear. "I'll try, but if I get eaten I will never forgive you!"

Chapter Fifteen

Saturday morning, Tails snuck out of the house through the window in Ilove's bedroom. She had left it opened just enough for her to get through. The sun was just beginning to rise. Nervously, she set out. Ilove had described the spot where she needed to meet the fairies. By the creek, on the grassy spot near the fallen tree. Look for Mr. Bunny or Mrs. Robin for directions if needed.

"I'M ON A SECRET MISSION TO HELP ILOVE! I'M ON A SECRET MISSION TO HELP ILOVE! I'M ON A SECRET MISSION TO HELP ILOVE!" Tails screamed as she ran. Thinking that if she was loud enough even the mean owl would hear her and leave her alone. She took cover behind every tall blade of grass or flower stem along the way.

"Shh! Why are you being so loud? I have little ones trying to sleep! I'm sure I'm not the only one! Can you keep it down?" shouted Mrs. Robin.

"Oh! I'm sorry! I didn't think about sleeping babes. I was more worried about being eaten!" cried Tails.

"Why are you out here if you are so afraid? Go back home or be quiet!" Mrs. Robin ruffled her feathers and went back to tending to her chicklets.

"I'm on a secret mission for Ilove." Tails loudly whispered up.

"Not much of a secret with you yelling like that! What mission? Where is Ilove? I haven't seen her for days. I usually eat my dinner with her. She always finds the best clover." Mr. Bunny mumbled.

"She has to stay home when she gets home from school. Ilove told her mother everything and she didn't believe her. She thinks she is making everything about the fairies up. So as punishment, she is forbidden to come to the woods until she learns her lesson about lying. I have to let the fairies know. She is supposed to go with them today to see if she can help them with their friends." Tails panted out. She hasn't had to run this much since she made her home inside Ilove's closet.

"Oh no!" Mr. Bunny declared. "How I have missed her! I hope she gets to come back soon. All I've had to eat are daisy stems. I so miss the clover."

"Stop thinking about yourself, Mr. Bunny! Ilove is in trouble. She is being punished for lying when she is telling the truth!" Mrs. Robin admonished. "How can we help Tails?"

"Ilove described the meeting spot to me. I would be ever so grateful if one of you could show me. I'm terribly afraid I'll be in the wrong spot, just waiting. Waiting to meet the fairies or be eaten! Whichever happens first?" Tails exclaimed.

"I'll show you." Mr. Bunny said. "Mrs. Robin is busy with her little ones. I'm happy to help Ilove. Anyway, maybe I'll find some clover along the way."

Mrs. Robin rolled her eyes and flapped her wings at Mr. Bunny. He's impossible she thought.

"Oh! Thank you Mr. Bunny! I'll walk close to you. Hopefully, no one will see me and I won't get eaten after all!" Tails was ever so pleased to be out of danger. She couldn't wait to be back home and safe again.

"Hopefully, Ilove will get me some lovely cheese as a thank you. Wouldn't that be wonderful?" Tails thought to herself.

It didn't take long for the two of them to reach the meeting spot.

"Hmm... I don't see any clover but there are yummy looking lilacs over there. I'll be over there in case you need me." Off Mr. Bunny hopped. Nervously, Tails waited for the fairies. Ilove had neglected to tell her their names. She had no doubt that she would recognize them. I mean how many fairies could there be?

A short time later, three luminous dragonflies came to rest on the trunk of the fallen tree. Tails was getting more nervous by the second.

"Oh goodness! Where could they be? I hope I didn't miss them. Ilove would be so disappointed. No more cheese for me then!" Tails worried aloud.

The dragonflies looked at one another and started to become their true selves. Tails hid underneath some wide leaves of green plant. She didn't know what kind. She didn't care as long as it protected her from cats. Owls should be sleeping now. The bright colored lights frightened her even more. She didn't think she could be any more scared than she was at that moment. She peeked out and was suddenly amazed at the beautiful fairies standing before her.

"Hello, little one. What were you saying about Ilove?" Queen Gemeenah asked gently. "It's all right. You have nothing to be afraid of."

Tails slowly poked her head out from under the greenery.

"Ilove got in trouble with her mother. She is forbidden from the woods today. She asked that I let you know so that you wouldn't think that she stood you up on purpose. Ilove said to make sure you know that she wants to help you and your friends in any way she can. She wants go with you on the first Saturday that she is allowed." Tails blurted out all in a rush.

"Take a breath, little one. I understand. Please let Ilove know that we will return in the early morning of every Saturday until we meet again. We have waited many, many years for the chance to help our friends. We can wait a bit longer. Let her know how sorry we are that she got into trouble with her mother. I certainly hope it is not our fault." Queen Gemeenah said leaving in a flash of light.

Azure and Clover stayed behind.

"Do you know why Ilove got into trouble, little one? Inquired Azure.

"My name is Tails. Her mother was looking for her the day your Queen told her the story and asked for Ilove's help. When her mother couldn't find her, she panicked. Ilove's father went to war and never came back. I think her mother thought that she had lost Ilove too. When Ilove came home, she told her mother all that had happened, but her mother didn't believe her and punished her for making up stories. She is being punished for lying, even though she is telling the truth."

"What did her mother believe and not believe?" asked Clover.

"She believed Ilove was playing in the woods and lost track of time. She didn't believe the part about talking to fairies or having to help fairies on Saturday. She also said that she didn't really believe that Ilove could talk to animals. She told Ilove that she needed time away from the woods to get her head out of the clouds and to face reality. I don't know what that really means, but I don't think it's good." Tails explained.

"I see" was all Tails heard before both fairies took off in an explosion of blue and green light.

Chapter Sixteen

Two weeks had passed. Queen Gemeenah declared that no one was to interfere with Ilove's family troubles. The council for magical peoples agreed to allow Ilove to know of the existence of fairies only. Ilove is the only approved human, other than Edward of course. Azure and Clover were allowed to escort Ilove to Westfairland to help with the Unmoving Enchantment. The future of the relationship would be determined by whether or not Ilove was able to help. If Ilove turned out to be a descendant of Princess Iadore, the council will reconvene to review the "Ilove Situation".

"There is always a way to bend the rules." Clover suggested.

"True but the punishment..." whispered Azure.

"What did Ilove say? Pish posh! I miss our friends and Ilove seems cool!" Clover said defensively.

"As if... you only like her because she indulged her insanity about your name. Is that all it takes to win your friendship? Clov-ER?" Azure taunted.

"It is not that she indulged me! It is that she at least made an effort to understand and respect me. There is a difference. I know my name and what I am, but I feel differently than the rest of you. I do not feel like I belong. I am different and I know it. So does Ilove!" Clover stormed off. She had never expressed these feelings before out loud and she was mad at herself for doing so now. Azure is her best friend, but she did not seem to understand her. She longed to feel like she belonged. If that was too much to ask for, she would settle for being understood or at least accepted.

Azure felt terrible for having hurt Clover's feelings. She did not understand. She thought Clover was just going through a phase, wanting to stand out. Now, she realized that it was something else, something more to what Clover was feeling. Clover just needed her to be a better friend. She went looking for her to say she was sorry and to ask what she could do for her. How could she be a better friend?

She spotted Clover sitting and crying by Queen Isadora's resting place. The spot had become sacred to the fairies. It is the best place to go for a time out, for alone time. At first Azure did not know if she should bother her or not. She did not want to interrupt Clover's reverie. If she is here, she wants to be left alone.

"I know you are there. Can I not get a minute to myself?" Clover whined in a tear soaked voice.

"Absolutely. You do not have to say anything. I just want you to listen." Azure quietly approached. "I am very sorry. You are right. I did not understand. I would like to. I promise to listen." Then, she left Clover to her thoughts.

Clover found Azure in her room. She never liked it in here. All the flowers, pinkness, and overall cuteness made her skin feel itchy. Clover's own room was very sparse and drew on the darker colors found in nature.

"Ahem. Let us not turn this into a thing. We are good. I think I have found a way to help Ilove and keep us out of trouble. Interested?" Clover suggested as a peace offering.

Azure responded without any hesitation. "Am I ever?" She was thrilled that she was forgiven and already embroiled in an adventurous plot. "What do you have in mind?"

"Well, we are supposed to go to the woods every Saturday until we are able to bring Ilove back with us." Clover began. "What if her mother "accidentally" spotted one or both of us in our true form? Out of the corner of her eye, so to speak. Then, she would have to believe Ilove even if she is not quite sure of what she saw. She will have no proof and there would be no other witnesses. She would be afraid that people will think she has lost her senses which means she would not be likely to tell anyone else. But she would "know" what she saw. If nothing else, she should be willing to at least consider Ilove's stories about our existence. Ilove will be able to play in the woods again. Operation Free Our Friends will be back on! What do you think?"

"I think you are brilliant! Let us go watch the mother to find the right moment to put your plan into action!" Azure could not wait to begin. "Only one question, which one of us should she see?"

"Now that I think about it, why not let her see us both by accident? Two of us would be hard to disbelieve. I could pick a flower or something for you. She can see me give you the flower." Clover was excited for the plan. "I should have thought of this first."

"I like it!" Azure assured her.

The following Saturday morning, Ilove sat sadly in her room reading, while Clover and Azure watched Trailynn hang freshly washed laundry on a line to dry. She was humming a song that the fairies had not heard before. It was a lovely tune.

Azure and Clover looked at one another. The time had arrived.

Trailynn spotted bright colored lights on the edge of the woods. She was mesmerized when the lights turned into two...could those be fairies? Picking flowers? Just as suddenly the winged young ladies turned back into lights and disappeared.

"What did I just see?" Trailynn thought first. "Oh! Ilove!" was her second.

Chapter Seventeen

Trailynn could not believe what she had just seen. No matter how many times she tried to convince herself that it was just her imagination, she knew that what she saw was real. She saw two fairies picking flowers. No doubt about it. She saw them. They did not seem to be aware that she was there. No one would believe her.

Except for Ilove. Ilove was telling me the truth and I punished her for it. Great mothering there. I can't tell her either. I have a hard enough time getting her head out of the clouds and into the real world. If I tell her I punished her for no good reason, how could I ever discipline her again? How will I ever know if she is making something up or telling me the truth? Oh, no. What have I done? Now, what do I do?

"Ilove?" Trailynn called that evening before going to bed.

"Yes, mommy?" Ilove was still sullenly reading in her room all day. Occasionally, she looked wistfully out of her window at the woods she longed to be in. Tails had given her Queen Gemeenah's message. She no longer worried about disappointing the fairies. She only had to wait out her sentence.

"Ilove, honey. I'm sorry I got so angry the other day. I just got so scared when I couldn't find you. I love your imagination and your passion for the outdoors." Trailynn paused for a moment to collect her thoughts. "It's just that I worry so much. I also can no longer stand seeing the sadness on your face. Starting tomorrow, you can go back to play in the woods with your animal friends. I wish you played with other children, after school and homework of course. But, honestly, I'll be happier when you are happy. Plus, I'm sure the animals have missed you."

Ilove threw her arms around her mother.

"Oh, thank you, mommy! I have missed the woods so much! I promise I'll be back before dark and I won't go far. I'll try to be better at keeping track of the time. I love you so much!" Ilove gushed. She had her fingers crossed about the not going far part. Ilove didn't know where the fairy kingdom was located. She didn't think it was that far since the fairies seemed to make the trip easily enough. Yes they have wings, but they do not seem out of breath from flying. So, maybe it's not that far.

"I love you too!" Trailynn relished the warm enthusiastic hug from Ilove. "I look forward to hearing about your adventures. I have really missed your stories and I will try not to be so doubtful." She added a conspiratorial wink. "Get some sleep. I'm sure I won't see you for very long after school."

Her mother was right. As soon as Ilove got home from school, she raced to change into play clothes and ran to the woods. She called out to all her friends letting them know that she was back and how much she missed them.

"Hello, Mr. Bunny! How have you been?" Ilove asked. She knelt down to gently run her fingers through his soft gray fur and rubbed his ears just a bit.

"Tails told me of your troubles. Sorry 'bout that. I've missed the clover." Mr. Bunny said. He shivered with delight from the ear rub. "I mean you. I missed seeing you." He quickly corrected himself. No need to upset her. She may stop playing with my ears, he thought.

"Oh you! Clover! Clover! Clover! Don't you ever think about anything else?" Mrs. Robin scolded Mr. Bunny. "Hello, dear. Lovely to see you. Have you been all right?" Mrs. Robin had turned her attention to Ilove.

"Oh, yes! I'm fine. I did a lot of reading in my room. How are your little ones?" Ilove asked.

"See for yourself." Mrs. Robin looked to her chicklets and fluttered one wing. At the gesture, four little feather heads popped up to peer at Ilove over the edge of the nest.

"Oh my! They have gotten so big! I don't seem to understand them. What are they saying?"

"Nonsense. Just like all little ones at this age." Mrs. Robin explained. "It's non-stop nonsense these days."

Ilove chuckled and took a deep breath with her eyes closed. It was so wonderful to be home. This is where I belong. Opening her eyes, she spotted some clover for Mr. Bunny.

"There's some clover over by that oak tree, Mr. Bunny. It's in the shade, just like you like it." Ilove wondered why he couldn't find clover without her.

"Clover is sweeter in the shade, but it is sweetest when you are near." Mr. Bunny said. "That's how I really like it."

Ilove blushed. "That's how I like it too. Have you seen the fairies? I hope they still want my help. Can you imagine going to a fairy kingdom?"

"I've been seeing them every Saturday. Will you be here on Saturday? Come early." Mr. Bunny mumbled out in between bites of clover.

"Good to know. I brought my book. Want me to read to you?"

"I would. I have missed the stories terribly." Mr. Bunny replied.

Ilove walked over to the tree to sit leaning against the trunk and she began to read aloud. Animals from all over the woods began to gather around to listen, including two gem-colored dragonflies resting on a branch just above her head, sapphires and emeralds glittering in the sunlight.

Trailynn was also in the audience. She had followed Ilove on this sunny afternoon to discover what she enjoyed so much about being in the woods. She recalled Ilove's claims about talking to animals and reading to them, but the scene before her was an unexpected awe inspiring sight. Wow! She is truly magical. While she watched her Ilove entertain the woodland creatures, Trailynn also kept a watchful eye out for the fairies. She longed to see them again.

Chapter Eighteen

Saturday morning came and the sun had barely risen before Ilove jumped out of bed to race to the woods. She could barely contain her excitement for the adventure of the day. The fairy kingdom was waiting! Her imagination had been running wild for days. There she sat on the fallen tree by the creek anxious and patient. She was boiling over with excitement.

She did not have to long to wait.

Azure and Clover zoomed by her several times while performing some astounding aerial feats to express their elation at Ilove's return. When their tiny dragonfly celebration was done, they flashed into their fairy selves.

"Hello, Ilove! I have missed you!" Clover gushed.

"Hello, Cloven! I have missed you too! You have no idea how I have missed the woods, my animal friends, and, of course, both of you. I know we have just met, but I so look forward to getting to know you both better. I have so much to learn! How is Queen Gemeenah?" Ilove's enthusiasm was contagious.

"You can ask her yourself in a flash." Azure said.

"Oh, so it's not far then?"

"I mean we will be travelling by light." Azure took Ilove's hand.

Ilove did not have words for how her body felt. Weightless was the only word that came to mind. How does a person describe being a ball of blue light? The opposite edge of the woods was fast approaching and the mountains beyond were coming into view. Ilove had heard of the mountains beyond the woods, but had never seen them. She had suddenly realized that she had not travelled this far from home before. This thought made her afraid for a moment. She knew that she was safe with the fairies. She had nothing to fear, but still, she was now very far from home.

About half way up the mountain, Ilove noticed a cave.

In her head she heard Azure's voice, "The cave is an entrance to a series of tunnels that lead to our cavern and our kingdom, Westfairland. It's the most beautiful of all the fairy lands in my opinion."

"You only say that because you have never been to another fairy land." Clover chided.

"No harm in having pride in your homeland and I say that because ours is the only fairy kingdom with humans!" Azure shot back.

Ilove was amused by their banter as she tried to focus on the view. Everything was going by so fast. She tried to believe that she was the first person to ever see the world from this viewpoint, but she knew that wasn't true. Surely, there have been others and that's all right. This is still pretty amazing! Without warning, they plunged into the near darkness of the cave system. The tunnels were beginning to seem endless when the trio burst into cavern. They settled in the middle of the village where Roman once regaled the villagers with the stories of his adventurous travels. Ilove felt a bit woozy after regaining her true form.

She stood braced between Azure and Clover.

"That will take a bit of getting used to." Ilove gasped.

Both of the fairies giggled.

"That is what King Roland said the first time I took him to my sitting room." Queen Gemeenah laughed. She had noticed their arrival and came down to greet Ilove. "It is an adjustment, but you will get used to it."

Ilove was looking around with wide eyes, taking in all of the Unmoving people. All were locked in place mid-task. A few were being dusted by some fairies. What a strange sight. So many questions were bouncing around in her head she did not know which to ask first, so she asked none.

Queen Gemeenah seemed to understand instinctively.

"Come with me and I will do my best to explain."

Ilove followed Queen Gemeenah to King Roland's home. There he sat on his modest throne, the very picture of royal despair. A tear rolled down Ilove's cheek at the sight of him and yet she could not quite explain why. She *felt* so much love from him and so much sadness in him. This was like nothing she had ever experienced before.

"This is King Roland. We were, are very good friends. I know I told you the story, but now you have a face to put with the name. He came from a long, long line of great kings. He had a very greedy and selfish twin brother. He and his twin were the first set of twins in their lineage. Roland was the first and Richard was the second. Roland became King and Richard was a Prince. This drove Richard to madness and war that divided their kingdom. When King Roland and Queen Isadora discovered that a royal child was on the way, they decided to leave to find a new peaceful kingdom to raise their child. They feared how Richard would react and did not want their child to live in a time of war. Many of their people who were also tired of Richard's antics left with them. Eventually, they found this cavern. Originally, they were only going to stay long enough to rest and then they were going to move on.

"Then, the whole group decided to stay. At that time, none of the humans were aware that the fairy folk already lived here. Once I learned that the humans had planned to stay. I made our presence known. What a shock that was! King Roland and I went to my sitting room to get to know each other. Fairies knew of humans from long ago and nothing that we knew was good. The humans that we had known were more like Prince Richard, you see. King Roland is much different. Prince Richard is greedy and mean. King Roland is generous and good.

"I agreed to share the cavern with the humans until the child was born. I then showed the humans the real cavern. What you see now I mean. When they arrived, the cavern was empty. It was all darkness with just a small stream of water. No flowers or fruit. No fish. No animals. I wanted it to be as uninviting as possible so they humans would want to leave. Once I understood King Roland's intentions and I knew true his heart. Well, that night I cast a spell on the humans connecting King Roland to his people. This meant that if King Roland wanted peace and harmony then his people would want peace and harmony. If King Roland was happy then his people would be happy. At the time I thought I was ensuring that I was preventing another Prince Richard type war. You have to remember that I had not had any previous experience with humans and I had not even heard any good stories.

"I had no way of knowing what was to come." Queen Gemeenah paused as she stroked King Roland's cheek as if she were wiping away an imaginary tear. "Queen Isadora was not well. She had become very weak. We did not know why. The mid wives and all of us were doing all that could be done, but nothing was working. She rested and took nourishment. We all thought that she would eventually recover once the baby was born. On the night of the delivery, Violet, you will meet her later, sensed that Queen Isadora was going to leave this world. She and I came down to ease her passing. We brought the child into the world. A girl. The midwives tended to the infant while Violet tended to Queen Isadora. Then, Violet had to take over care of the baby. Queen Isadora was no more.

"King Roland was inconsolable. *ALL* of the humans were inconsolable. For days and days. Their weeping was endless. The sadness consumed them. I knew it was because of the spell that I had cast. I had to snap King Roland out of his despair so that the rest of his people would also come to their senses. Once a spell like that is cast, it cannot be undone. The infant. She saved us all. He named her Iadore. And she was adored by us all. King Roland insisted that she be educated in both human and fairy ways. Her curiosity was had no bounds and also the root cause of our current situation. She loved to go on what she called "mini adventures". On one such adventure, she fell from a great height and pierced her heart on a bit of jagged rock. That is when I shared my fairy light with her to restore her to life.

"She became a half fairy, as much my child as King Roland's. On her last adventure, she got lost in the tunnels and never to return or be found. King Roland's grief was so deep that he shut down completely. His people were still connected to him. They also shut down. I cast another spell to lock them in the moment, to freeze the people as they are to preserve them in their current state until the princess found. It has been too many years for the princess to still be alive. I know this. But, you see, her fairy light never returned to me. This means that she had a child that she passed the light onto. That child had a child and so on. I believe you are Iadore's descendant and now have my fairy light. I believe that you have the ability to break the spell and restore Westfairland's humans.

"Do you understand all that I have said? I know I told the story before, but this time I gave you more details and you are actually here to see the truth of it all. Do you have any questions for me?" Queen Gemeenah waited while Ilove collected her thoughts. She could see Ilove working through everything she had been told.

"I do have a few questions. Do you mean to say that I am half fairy?" Ilove asked. "And can all fairies cast spells? I thought only witches could cast spells? Are witches even real?" Ilove fired off these questions with barely a breath in between.

"Not quite. With each generation the fairy light is weakened, but it is still there. You have displayed the same fairy gifts that Iadore had. She too could talk to animals and make plants grow bigger. If you were truly a half fairy the spell would have broken the second you walked in. No, only Fairy Queens can cast spells and usually with help, but I am not permitted to say help from who. I am Queen here, but I am part of a larger council. I am only allowed to share with you this information pertaining to Westfairland and the Unmoving Enchantment. If it turns out that you are in fact a descendant of Iadore, the council will decide then what more I may share with you."

"Oh! So witches exist! You just can't confirm it! Got it!" Ilove said with a conspiratorial wink. "If I'm not a half fairy, but only a descendant, does that mean that I cannot break the spell? Since the fairy light that I have is too weak?" Ilove looked down disappointed.

"Oh no, dear. I still believe you are Princess Iadore's descendant. I just think the fairy light is weakened by the generations. I honestly do not know how you can break the spell. I just know that only you can. I wish I knew better how to guide you. What I would like ask of you is if you are willing to continue to try? My thoughts are for you to talk to King Roland. About absolutely anything you would like. Princess Iadore used to prattle on about all kinds of nonsense and he would relish just listening to her. Maybe over time your words will get through and the enchantment will break. I think it will just take time."

"I will do all that I can." Ilove promised.

Chapter Nineteen

Ilove came to Westfairland every Saturday. She would sit and talk to King Roland. She had also begun to help the fairies with maintaining the rest of the humans in Westfairland. Queen Gemeenah allowed her to roam free. She delighted in watching Ilove express her curiosity and delighted in how much Ilove reminded her of Iadore. Marigold volunteered to tutor her in fairy ways. She was an eager student.

One bright Saturday Ilove came across a young man building a table. Ilove was surprised by this. He was not Unmoving!

"Ah, hello?" Ilove said tentatively.

"Hello yourself. I'm Edward. You must be Ilove?" Edward stated. He was a very nice looking young man with a very disarming smile. Ilove didn't know what to do. She was caught completely off guard. She was used to the idea that she was the only human in Westfairland that was not Unmoving. So who was this guy?

"Confused by me? No one told you about me? Well I'm a bit of a story? Violet is my fairy mother. Are you interested? Or do you have to go? Have you now become one of the Unmoving?" Edward was teasing Ilove a bit. She was clearly stunned speechless and he couldn't resist.

"I, um, who are you again? And why aren't you Unmoving?" Ilove managed.

"I am Edward and I came after the enchantment. So I missed out on being Unmoving. Whew!" Edward wiped his hand across his brow in a mock gesture of wiping non-existent sweat away. "Lucky me!"

"How did you get here?" Ilove asked.

"How did you get here? Actually, don't answer that. I already know all about you. Well, sort of. You are the talk of all Westfairland. Any luck with the King?" Edward replied. "Oh, and my story is a bit long."

"Um, no luck with the King and I have all day."

"Well, all right then. Have a seat."

Ilove sat on a nearby stool. Edward waved his hand and some flowers cups grew already filled with nectar.

"Comfy? All right. A long time ago, I actually do not know how long I have been here or how long I was lost before I found Woody, I lived in a small cottage on the edge of town by great woods. I was very happy there. My father worked at a lumber mill. My mother stayed at home. She taught me to read and write. She was very afraid to let me venture out of her sight. Turns out she was right to be afraid. She was awfully afraid of dust and dirt. She cleaned constantly. I had to have a bath every morning and every night. I played only inside. I had to be terribly good all the time.

"Don't get me wrong. I loved both of my parents very much. I just longed for some adventure. I wanted run and play outside. My father would try to convince my mother that I needed fresh air. I needed dirt under my nails. I needed to climb trees. My mother would hear none of it. All she heard was dirt and injuries. She would always reply "Maybe when he's a little older".

"One day I woke up from an afternoon nap to find that my mother was still asleep. This was the first time that had ever happened. I saw this as an opportunity to step outside. I told myself that I would just cross the threshold and be right back before she ever found out. My heart was racing. Pure thunder in my chest. I was born in that house. I don't think I had ever been outside of it for even a second. I was both excited and terrified at the same time. For a moment, the fear almost won. Then, I thought it might not get another chance. So out I went. Once I was out the door, there was no going back!

"The outside world was full of smells and color and textures and wonders and I started running around looking and touching and smelling everything and before I knew it I was deep in the woods with no idea where I was or how to get home. I called out for my mother. I yelled out for my father. Then I just screamed for any one at all to hear me, to save me. I started to run, but I didn't know in what direction I was running or where I was running to. Remember this was the first time I had ever been outside much less in the woods. I went from being thrilled and excited to being frightened and terrified.

I started to cry because I had lost all hope that I would find my way home. I feared that I would never see my parents again. I fell down so many times. Tripped over tree roots and low branches hit my head, scratched my arms. I was covered in dirt and grime. Everything that my mother imagined that might happen was actually happening to me and worse. I was covered scrapes and bruises, little cuts. This had gone on for days. I was so hungry and the thirst! I was just stumbling about at this point. Then I spotted a large hole in the base of a tree. It was the biggest tree I had come across yet. I decided I could squeeze myself into this hole for a bit of sleep. I thought I would be safe in there. Sheltered somewhat, you see."

Edward paused in his reverie to make sure that Ilove was keeping up with his story. He clearly had her full attention. She was hanging on his every word. With a slight nod, he continued.

"When I woke up, I was in a completely different forest, but for some strange reason I was no longer afraid. That part I cannot explain. I don't know how I knew I was safe. I just did. These woods were not dark or scary. The flowers were somehow more beautiful and in colors that I did not know even existed. There were waterfalls and rainbows and dragonflies and birds and butterflies. I mean the very air was filled with moving explosions of color. The trees were loaded with every kind of fruit. The birds seemed to sing melodies instead of chirping. The only unkind sound was my grumbling stomach. I reached up to grab an apple of a branch. I was so hungry!"

"Ouch! You could at least ask! How rude!"

"I looked around to see who had said that. I wanted to apologize for stealing the apple. I knew that once I explained my situation, everything would be all right and I would be given the apple. Only to discover that it was the tree that had spoken. I then did the only sensible thing. I fainted! I went right out straight away!"

Ilove busted out laughing. Edward smiled back. He laughed too.

"I'm sorry for laughing. I probably would have fainted too if a tree talked to me. Thank you for letting me know such a thing is even possible." Ilove said. Her laughter only grew.

"It is possible indeed in the magical woods that I found myself in. You see, the tree that I crawled into was a Creeping Willow. His name is Woody. We have since become very good friends."

Ilove shook her head, "Don't you mean a Weeping Willow?"

"Oh, no. They are distant cousins. Twice removed I believe. I know it's all very confusing. Should I continue?"

Ilove nodded eagerly.

"When I came to, I was surrounded by all sorts of creatures talking all at once. Some to me but most were talking about me. There was a pile of fruit next to me. Woody had explained where he had found me and let them know that I was lost in the woods with no home. While I was passed out, the magical folk had been busy cleaning me up. They had mended my wounds and my clothes as best as they could. I told them that I did have a home and it was a really great one. I just didn't know where it was. They said that I was welcome to stay in the magical woods with them, but sadly there was no way for me to get home. None of them knew how to find my home either. Woody had found me in the middle of the mystic woods. These are the woods that connect the regular human woods and the magical woods. I had wandered very, very far.

"The down side to the magical realms is that there is no sense of time. I have no idea how long I was there or here for that matter. I was about nine when I got lost. I think. I am obviously not that now, but I do not know how old I actually am. I learned many, many things there."

"How did you end up in Westfairland and with Violet? Ilove interrupted.

"Right. That bit of the story. Well, one day I was playing by one of the waterfalls and Manbug sent me to look for leprechaun treasure at the end of the one of the rainbows. I..."

"Excuse me, but who? Did you say Manbug?" Ilove thought to herself that this had to be good. Seriously. Manbug?

"Yes, Manbug. He's another friend of mine that I met in the magical woods. He's a little red round bug with black spots."

"Like a ladybug." Interrupted Ilove.

"Exactly! That's what I thought and said! But as it turns out he's a "he" and was very offended when I called him a her! It turned into a whole thing! We have since become friends and we laugh about it now, but at first wow! It was a good lesson for me though. Never assume anything about any one based on how they look! Get to know them for who he or she is and go from there. Anyway, Manbug told be about the treasure and I went looking for it. I fell into the water. I almost drowned. I got very sick. None of the magical folk there could help me. Woody was afraid that I was going to die, so he brought me here. Queen Gemeenah confirmed his suspicion that I was near death. She could do nothing for me because she had given half of her light to Princess Iadore. So Violet stepped up to help me.

"Violet also missed the humans. She said even though she knew that I could not break the Unmoving Enchantment, she knew that I could at least remind them of the humans they all missed so dearly. Afterwards, I chose to stay in Westfairland. I do go to visit the magical woods to see my friends from time to time. And that my dear is my story." Edward gave a little bow to demonstrate that his story was done.

Ilove clapped and then gasped.

"What?" Edward asked. He wondered if there was some part of the story that he had forgotten.

"I think my mother and I live in your old cottage. The kids at school always tease me that our cottage is haunted because a boy that used to live there went missing a long, long time ago. I never believed them. I thought they were just making it up to tease me. I guess now I know the truth." Ilove confessed.

"A long, long time ago?" Edward looked very sad. "Any idea what happened to my parents?"

"No. I'm sorry. I really didn't believe the taunts until just now." Ilove felt bad for even mentioning this. "I promise to go to the library to see what I can find out if you would like."

"Yes. I believe I would." Edward said. After a moment. "Actually, on second thought, no. I have always wanted to believe that they lived happily ever after. I hoped that they missed me but lived happily together and found some sort of peace with my disappearance. Maybe, they even had another child. I do not know that I can live knowing anything differently."

"I think understand" Ilove replied in a hushed tone. She could tell he was remembering his parents, missing them. She didn't not want to disturb his reverie.

Chapter Twenty

Monday after school, Ilove stopped by the library to look up old newspaper stories about Edward's disappearance. She explained her interest to the librarian by explaining the taunts and then the discovery that the disappearance was real. She, of course, left out the bit about actually meeting Edward. She said that since she now lived in the very same cottage she wanted to write a school report on the effects of that Edward's disappearance may have had on his parents.

The librarian thought it was an interesting topic. This was the first time that she could remember ever being asked for information about Edward's incident or the aftermath. The two of them searched for hours. Edward had been missing for about eighty years. Ilove thought that was interesting. He only looks about fifteen or so. Two of them found tons of articles on the search for Edward. At first, the constable thought that he had been stolen, but there was no evidence to support that.

Upon further investigation, Edward's footprints were found and tracked. It was obvious to the trackers in the initial search parties that he had gone into the woods on his own and gotten lost. It was then reported that his mother blamed herself for Edward's disappearance. She first blamed herself for falling asleep and then blamed herself for not allowing him to go outside. Through it all, his father stood by her. He did not blame her at all because he knew she loved him and did everything for him with the best intentions. The newspapers also confirmed that Edward was in fact ten years old at the time of his disappearance.

Eventually, the search had been called off. Nobody had ever been found (obviously Ilove thought) and it was the belief that Edward was taken in by one of the caravans to be raised in new community in the West. Well, as it turned out, they were not entirely wrong, Ilove thought. That belief was a comfort to his parents, who remained together for the rest of their lives. They did not have any more children. His parents always held out the hope that when Edward grew up he would find his way home. Ilove made copies of all the articles and made a scrap book for Edward when she got home.

At long last Saturday arrived and Ilove could hardly wait to get to Westfairland. She felt she had a great deal to share with King Roland. Azure and Clover had come to the woods nearly every day this week. As it turns out, they also enjoyed listening to her read books out loud. Ilove enjoyed performing all kinds of funny character voices as she read. She thrived on hearing the giggles from her audience. Mrs. Robin's little ones had all grown and were off to find their own adventures. She has been a little sad as of late, so Ilove chose to read a funny story this week about silly monkey named George.

This day, however, began differently than all the previous Saturdays. Instead of heading straight to King Roland, today Ilove went to find Edward first.

"You know, I just realized I neglected to ask you what you were building when we met last week. I also just now realized that you are actually *building* something instead of using a fairy gift. Why is that?" Ilove walked up and just continued their conversation as if a week had not passed in between the sentences.

"I'm building furniture for my cottage there." Edward pointed to a small, cute house by the stream not far from where he was working. "I love to build because it keeps me connected to the fact that I am human, not fairy. Well, at least, I started out as human. Yes, I have some fairy gifts that I use and enjoy, but I enjoy the sense of accomplishment I feel when I make something of use with my hands as well. Take this table for example. I carve all these designs myself. It is my art and it gives me a sense of purpose. I realize you are young, so I don't know if this makes sense to you." Edward looked away as if his admissions to her were embarrassing to him.

"Actually, I think I do understand. I feel more at home in the woods talking and reading to animals than I do with other people or even being in the cottage with my mother. I do not really seem to like other people very much or at least most of them." Ilove blushed deeply. "I've never said that out loud before."

Edward laughed. "Your secret is safe with me. What have you got there?"

"Oh, this is the reason I came to see you. It is a present and a mystery for you. It is entirely your choice to open it or not. I won't mind either way. I went to the library as I said I would. I did research on your disappearance. I, also, found out what happened to your parents. I put all the articles I found together a scrap book for you. I did a school report on it, too. I hope you don't mind on that part, but I got an "A" if that helps. It's just that I had to do a report on something and I spent so much time doing research on you that I didn't have any time to do research on anything else. So, ah, sorry if that bothers you. But, well, here it is." With that, Ilove left the scrap book, tied with ribbon on the table and turned to run away.

"Wait!" Edward yelled. Ilove stopped. She didn't turn around out of fear of his reaction to what she had done.

"Thank you." At first this is all Edward can say. He was not sure of what he was feeling. It seemed that several very long, awkward minutes had passed could say anything else. "I made something for you as well. Please do not turn around. I'm sorry. I'm just a little off at the moment."

Ilove could hear emotion in Edward's voice, but she did not know if it sadness or anger. She remained facing away from him. She felt something be placed upon her head.

"Iadore's full name was Princess Iadore Daisy. Her father King Roland added Daisy as a second name to honor the fairy folk. Before, humans only went by a first and last name. She would have been just Princess Iadore, but she was special and she was also Daisy. Maybe, he somehow knew when she was born that she would eventually be a half fairy. I don't know. The dwarf king, King Mineguard, had an enchanted crown of daisies especially made for her. Now, this little crown is not enchanted and it is not made of gemstones, but I did carve it especially for you. I hope you like it. I believe that you are also very special."

Ilove reached up to touch the crown. She took it off to get a good look at it. The carvings were delicate and intricate. Somehow, the crown shone as if it were made of some sort of gemstones instead of just wood. It was absolutely the most beautiful thing she had ever seen. She turned to say so, but Edward and the scrap book were gone.

Replacing the crown on her head, wiping a tear from her cheek, Ilove set off to tell King Roland about her week. Walking through Westfairland, Ilove waved and called out to her fairy friends. She surprised herself in doing so. At home, I never would have done such a thing she thought.

She was also thinking over her encounter with Edward just now. Two things were bouncing around in her head. One, Edward thought she was special. And two, did he say dwarf king? Now, there are dwarves. Of course, there are. Any day now, there will be unicorns. I'm special and there are dwarves. And the day just got started.

"What a week!" Ilove exclaimed, plopping down in the comfortable chair Queen Gemeenah provided for her. "First, school. Enough said there! The best part about that is that I had to do a report on any subject for history. As it turns out, I live in the same cottage that Edward lived in before he disappeared. Do you know Edward? He lives here now. He is Violet's fairy god child? He lived with Woody the Creeping Willow in the magical wood?" Ilove looked up to search King Roland's face for any sign of change. Screamed!

"EEEEAAAA!!! Your eyes are watching me! You didn't move your head, but your eyes moved! And there is a twinkle! Wait! And your lips are slightly curved on one side! You know Edward? No! You can't! He came after! Do you know me then? Do you recognize me?" Ilove kept firing questions. Her mind was racing. King Roland did not move, but had definitely changed.

Queen Gemeenah, Violet, Azure, Clover, Marigold, and countless other fairies came rushing into King Roland's home at Ilove's scream. All hoping that the enchantment had been broken, but knowing that it had not because all the others were still Unmoving. Then, they were gripped with fear that she had somehow been injured.

"What is it? Where are you hurt?" Queen Gemeenah demanded.

"I'm not hurt. I'm fine. But him! Look!" Ilove demanded, pointing at King Roland. "His eyes have MOVED! He is watching me. And look at his mouth, is he smiling a bit?" Ilove indicated all the changes she noticed. Just then, everyone in the room gasped, as King Roland moved his index finger to point back at Ilove.

It had taken some time, but could the Unmoving Enchantment be breaking at long last?

Queen Gemeenah looked strangely at Ilove, noticing the wooden daisy crown for the time.

"Where did you get that?" she whispered.

"Edward made it for me. He told me the story of Princess Iadore and how she got her middle name Daisy to honor of the fairies. My middle name is Riley. It honors my mother's family. My father named me Ilove because when I was born the first thing he said to me was 'I love you'. He said he want me to know that he loved me every time he said my name." Ilove explained all this as if in a trance, not taking her eyes off of King Roland for a second. "My full name is Ilove Riley Kingston."

Queen Gemeenah nodded. Then, she nodded her head toward King Roland, "That is strangely similar to how and why he named the Princes Iadore. I was there. It was the first thing he said to her. I adore you. Then, he said that is your name Princess Iadore. Dandelion made a baby blanket for Princes Iadore, pink with daisies on it. She was wrapped in the blanket. He looked at me, smiled and said Princess Iadore Daisy. Fairies, we take our names from nature based on the color of our inner light." She paused, "I think it was the sight of you with the crown that jogged his memory to *really* see you and hear you for the first time. Are you all right to keep going?"

"Yes. I'm okay now. Just scared me at first. Caught me off guard a bit. I'm fine now." Ilove stammered.

"Understandable." Queen Gemeenah laughed. "It would have scared me, too. Please, let me know immediately if there are any more changes, preferably with a little less screaming if possible. If not, like I said, it is understandable."

Every one left Ilove alone with King Roland as she settled into her place for the second time that day.

Chapter Twenty One

As Ilove continued her weekly update with King Roland, everyone else had gone to see if any of the other people had made any subtle changes. She moved her chair a few times to do an "eye test" on King Roland, testing to see if he was really "watching" her. His eyes never appeared to leave her.

"Well, then, seems like I certainly have your undivided attention." Ilove nervously laughed. "Where did you so rudely interrupt me?" She chuckled. "Oh, right, Edward. So as it turns out Edward has a bit of a long story that you don't know anything about, but let's just say he's a guy that lives here and he's a half fairy like Princess Iadore, your daughter. Before he lived here, he lived in the house that I live in now. It has been this huge town mystery about his disappearance and I did a report on it. Of course, I can't be like "Hey I found him!" That would not be good at all. I went with the theory that he got lost in the woods and was picked up by one of the travelling caravans' theory."

"Which, when you think about it, isn't too far from the truth, if you leave out all the magical bits. I got copies of all the articles and made a scrap book for Edward as a present. He said that he often wondered what happened to his parents after he disappeared. Then he said he wanted to know and didn't want to know at the same time. I told him that the he now had the information. He could find out if and when he was ready. Added bonus, I got an "A" on the report. That's really good if you don't know what that means. He made me this crown. He said that you named your daughter Princes Iadore Daisy and since I am her descendant, I deserved a crown. He said he thinks I'm special. I don't know about all that.

"My name is Ilove though. I told Queen Gemeenah how my father came up with my name and she said it was very close to the way you came up with Iadore's name. And now, I have a similar crown. I know that mine is not made of gemstones and I have not seen the original crown, but this one is the most beautiful crown I have ever seen. What do you think?" Ilove looked up from drawing on random piece a paper, a habit that she had developed to pass the time while talking to the King, and had to stifle another scream. King Roland had turned his head to face her.

"Look, I'm all for breaking your Unmoving Enchantment and all, but we've got to find a way for you to make some sort of noise or something. These little bits of silent movement are freaking me out. No offense, but seriously." Ilove took a deep breath to calm herself. Shaking her head a bit as if to clear away the heebie jeebies. "I'll be right back. Hold that thought." She giggled to herself as she walked out of King Roland's house.

Ilove initially went outside to look for Azure and Clover to see if they had any ideas about how to get King Roland to make some sort of noise when he makes tiny movements, but was immediately stopped in her tracks when she saw all the commotion in the cavern. There were explosions of activity everywhere her eyes could see. All of the humans had moved in some slight way. She spots Azure on the platform in the center of the village. She was slowly turning in small circles, appearing to take in everything that was happening around her. Ilove headed her way.

"In all my life, I have not seen this much going on. I heard all the stories of King Roland, Rowan, the festivals, all of it, but all I have ever known is changing. It is what we, I, have always wanted. It is all happening now because of you." Azure said this to Ilove without looking at her, knowing that she was listening. "I do not know what to think or how to feel. Every day has been the same and now or, at least very soon, every day will be unexpected. Should I thank you?" Azure furrowed her brow, confusion clearly visible in her expression.

"I don't know either honestly. I was looking for you though. King Roland moved his head. I agree the Enchantment is breaking. It's slow though. Here's the thing, it's freaking me out. Scaring me. I know it's not supposed to, but I'm so used to him *not* moving and then he's staring at me with this odd expression on his face. Well, it just freaks me out! So I was wondering if you could help me like I don't know, put a bell on him or something that lets me know he moved so it doesn't scare me when I look up and he's staring at me." Ilove blurted this all out in one breath, as if she were as embarrassed by the admission as she was by the suggested solution.

Azure looked at her for a moment, as if she had not understood a word. Then, she burst into laughter. This time, Ilove furrowed her own brow.

"Please, don't laugh at me. Did you see the way he was staring at me? Tell me that it isn't unnerving? I even tried moving my chair around. It's creepy." Ilove said defensively.

"I am sorry. I am not laughing at you. Honestly. I just had an image of King Roland with little bells all over him and well, it was funny. Then I pictured him with one giant bell on his head. Just the images that flashed through my mind were terrible and *funny*. I, also, believe I understand what you are trying to say. All of these people are different ever so slightly than they were before. This is an entirely new sight for me! For example, you see that man over there, his right foot has been resting on the bottom rail of that fence for my entire life and now look at it. It is on the *grass*! I know that is not very impressive, but that is just one man!

All of them have changed. That is just the beginning. That means the more that King Roland moves the more the rest of them will move, until the Enchantment is completely broken. LIFE will return to this cavern. The festivals will begin again. Everything that once was, will be again. This is absolutely the most exciting day in my life! I have known all of these people my entirely life and yet I know nothing about them. Yet!"

"And I couldn't be happier for you! I'll be happy continue to talk to King Roland and do all that I can to finish waking him up, but if I have a heart attack from him scaring me to death all will be lost!" Ilove said a little more sarcastically than she meant. "Any ideas how we can prevent that last bit."

"Yes! Of course! I am sorry!" Azure was laughing at Ilove this time. She was full of hope and joy like never before. She was experiencing many new emotions for the first time.

Back in King Roland's house, Azure had placed tiny bluebell flowers about his head and hands.

"There these should take care of the problem." Azure said.

"Really? They are lovely and he looks very pretty, but how are flowers going to help? I mean he does look a bit less scary. I'm not sure that is going to be enough to *not* freak me when he moves." Ilove cautioned.

"No, silly. These are bluebells. In your world, these are just pretty flowers to look at. Here, well, there is a reason they are called bluebells. They are blue, yes, and they are bells. We use them in our music as instruments." Azure waved a hand and then flicked one of the bluebells with her index finger. A melodic tinkling sound followed that reminded Ilove of the wind chimes her mother hung outside the kitchen window. "The slightest movement will create a sound to alert you."

"Thank you. That is amazing and beautiful." Ilove looked at Azure. "I'm sorry I doubted you. I shouldn't have. Now, I can't wait for the first festival either!" Ilove winked to make sure that everything the gesture implied was being understood. Ilove was committed to break the Enchantment as she resumed her seat next to King Roland for the third time today.

Ilove talked for hours. Eventually, her chatter seemed to be set to music. Without realizing, she had lost track of time. The hour had grown very late.

Clover came to check on her out of concern. She remembered what happened the last time Ilove was out too late. When she told Ilove that it was almost gemlight, Ilove was also worried about the consequences. She told King Roland that it might be a few weeks before she could return, but she promised to do so.

Chapter Twenty Two

Clover brought Ilove to the edge of the woods by her house, as close as she dared before transforming them both back to their true forms. So fast, in fact, they both tumbled to the ground in a crash landing that resulted in a rolling stop in the tall grass.

"Oh, goodness! It's late in the day! My mother is going to be hopping mad! I hope to see you Saturday. If not, you'll know why!" Ilove yelled over her shoulder. Ilove looked up to see the sky quickly changing from being a riot of salmon and cantaloupe to the rich color of a violent bruise.

She burst through the back door of the cottage, "I'm so sorry, Mommy! Please don't be mad! I was reading and talking and I must have drifted off or something! I didn't even notice the dark! I swear!" Ilove was almost pleading with her mother. She searched her face for any sign that she believed her and that she would escape punishment.

Trailynn knew that Ilove was with the fairies. She didn't know where she *was* with the fairies, but she knew that she was safe with them. She had punished Ilove once before because she had not believed her when Ilove had tried to tell her the truth about the fairies. Ilove thought she was in trouble for being out after dark, not coming in when being called, and lying. She was out late and did not come back when she was called, but she was telling the truth.

She had seen two fairies herself, quite by accident while hanging laundry one day. There was no way to admit to Ilove that she had punished her lying when she wasn't or, at least, that is how she felt. So what does she do now? Confess? Admit that parents sometimes get it wrong? No, mustn't do that. Trailynn glanced out the window and a memory came to her. A way out had presented itself.

A smile came to her face.

"I don't doubt that you lost track of time. I don't pretend to understand your love for those woods. I know you feel more at home there than even here with me." Trailynn raised her hand to stop Ilove's attempt to protest. "It's all right. I'm not upset by this. This is not about love. I know you love me and I hope you know that I love you. This is something in your nature. It is who you are. Those woods are a part of you and that is all right. Tonight, though, there is another reason that you were not aware of the time or afraid of the dark. You see the moon. It is full. Very full. That, my sweet Ilove, is called a Super Moon. You can ask your teacher about it. However, if my grandmother, your great, grandmother were still around, she would tell you that the Man in the Moon was watching out for you."

"Who?" Ilove asked cautiously. Shaking her head as if she couldn't quite believe what was happening, Ilove then sputtered out a "What?" Did her mother know about a magical creature?

"Go get ready for bed and I will tell you the story that my grandmother told me about the man in the moon. I know you are wondering why I am not mad or punishing you. Call it resigned acceptance that the woods are your true home. I have come to realize I can either constantly fight with the tide or ride the wave. Understand?" Trailynn thought this was a pretty decent analogy without admitting anything.

"Not entirely, but if I'm not being punished or being told I can't go to the woods, I'll take it." Ilove rushed off to wash up for bed.

"Did you eat?" Trailynn called, trying to suppress a laugh. I'm just going to call this a mom win and move on.

Trailynn headed to the kitchen, then entered Ilove's bedroom with a glass of milk, a peanut butter & jelly sandwich, and a couple of cookies on a tray. Ilove looked at the tray with suspicion. "Who is this woman and what has she done with my mother?" Ilove thought.

Trailynn snickered at the look on Ilove's face.

"I promise this is not a trick of any kind. I'm really not mad and I'm really going to tell you a story while you eat. I prefer that you not make a habit out of being out so late. Once in a great while, I can handle. Deal?" Trailynn said with her hands in the air to gesture that she had nothing to hide.

"Deal." Ilove said, picking up her sandwich. PB&J, her favorite!

"All right, this is kind of long story. So get comfy." Trailynn began, reaching over to adjust Ilove's covers.

"A long, long, *long* time ago, there was only one land called Pangaea. The land was ruled by a King and Queen. When it became time for the King and Queen to retire, a pageant was held to find the new Queen. All the single young ladies that wanted to a chance to be Queen were allowed to compete. The ladies were judged based on their beauty, their talents in one of the arts, athletics, "

"That sounds like a beauty pageant." Ilove interrupted.

"Exactly. This is how beauty pageants got started. That is why beauty pageant winners are crowned and have courts. It is a tradition left over from these old customs. It has just been so long no one today even remembers how beauty pageants got started. Now, you do."

"Really! Wow! I had no idea!" Ilove exclaimed before taking a bite of a cookie.

"Of course! It's not like I'm making this stuff up!" Trailynn had to hide her face for a moment because she was in fact making it up. Her grandmother had never told any such story. She thought of using the moon as a way to explain why she wasn't mad instead of admitting that she knew about fairies. Oh, what a tangled web.

"Should I continue?" Trailynn asked with a raised eyebrow.

"Absolutely! Sorry!" Ilove was hanging on her every word. Her mother had never told her story from her great, grandmother before and this had started out to a really good one.

"Anyway, once the most beautiful, most talented, most intelligent and most athletic single young lady was crowned Queen, she was then required to hold a competition for all the single young men that wanted to a chance to be king. All the young men that wanted to compete were allowed to compete. Looks were not considered for the men. The potential kings were tested for bravery, weaponry, fighting skills, and such. There was first a series of games. You know, sword fights and jousts, that sort of thing. The winners became knights and the knights were sent on the final quest. The first knight to complete the quest became King. It was thought Pangaea would then ruled by the best possible King and the best possible Queen. The crown was earned, not inherited, you see.

"The system worked very well for many, many generations. Until one day, a queen wanted to rule forever with no king. She had heard rumors from the ancient wise ones that when the world was first created, there was the Tree of Knowledge and the Tree of Life. The first people knew they could never eat from either of these two Trees. They could eat the fruit from every other tree that grew in Pangaea and live forever in happiness. The fruit of these was forbidden. This is where the expression "Ignorance is Bliss" comes from. The people were happy, but they had no knowledge.

"Once the fruit of the Tree of Knowledge was eaten by the people of Pangaea, knowledge came to the people. That is why the times change, people change, and new technologies are invented. The people developed a hunger for knowledge and could no longer live in harmony. Seeing this, the Tree of Life was hidden. All feared the consequences of eating this forbidden fruit. The people tried to erase and forget all knowledge of the Tree of Life. But knowledge, being what it is, cannot ever be truly lost.

"The Forever Queen, as she became known, set the quest for the knights to find the Tree of Life. She believed eating this forbidden fruit would make her remain young and beautiful forever, hence the name. This way, she could reign for all time.

"All the knights fought bravely. All accepted the quest, but the Brave Knight fought hardest, but not because he wanted to be king. He did it because he truly loved the Forever Queen. He had always loved her, always had and always would. For as long as he could remember, since they were children together. He would not let her down. He gathered a group of squires and recruited a small army. He had consulted the ancient wise ones himself. He vowed to search every inch of Pangaea until he found the Tree of Life for his beloved. He would make her his true Queen.

"He searched for years and years. All his men were gone. He was the last knight still on the quest. He had no word from home. Yet, the Brave Knight persevered. Finally, the day had come. He had found the Tree of Life. He saw it in the distance in a beam of sunlight. It was like no other tree he had ever seen. There was a glow about the tree, a sort of aura. He headed for the tree. By now, he had grown old and weak.

"There! My beloved! I have done it! I will be home to you soon! My beloved! My Queen!" he rasped.

"Another step and the ground began to shake.

"NO! YOU MUST NOT TAKE FROM THE TREE OF LIFE! IT IS FORBIDDEN!" A loud booming voice seemed to fill the air. The Brave Knight could not see where the voice was coming from or who had spoken the words.

"I must! It is my destiny! It is for my love! It is for my Queen!" The Brave Knight shouted back.

"IS YOUR DESIRE TO BE KING SO GREAT THAT YOU WILL CONDEMN YOUR VERY SOUL?" The voice boomed.

"I care not about being King. I do not even care that she is Queen. I only care that she is the woman that I love and have loved every day that I have drawn breath. I do this for her, to win her hand and to earn her heart." The Brave Knight cried out. "She is my all."

"YOU HAVE FREE WILL! I CAN WARN YOU AGAINST YOUR ACTIONS! I CAN ADVISE YOU OF THE CONSEQUENCES! I CAN PUT BARRIERS IN YOUR WAY! YOUR CHOSEN PATH HAS NOT BEEN EASY! YOUR RETURN WILL BE EVEN HARDER!" The voice promised.

"The Brave Knight was not deterred one bit. He continued on his path towards the Tree of Life. His determination had not wavered for a second. He would bring back the fruit for his Queen!

"With that the ground shook even more violently than before. Just when the Brave Knight thought the shaking would never end, it did.

"He did not know what had happened. He thought to himself. A little ground shaking? That's all you got? No problem. I got this. The Brave Knight went to the Tree of Life and filled a satchel with forbidden fruit. Then, almost as an afterthought, he took some of the bark as well. Just in case. He did not know what part of the tree he was supposed to bring back. He also decided to take a small branch as well. This way he would have some leaves and sap for her as well. He waited for a few moments to see if there would be any more ground shaking or lightning strikes. Anything. There was nothing more.

"The Brave Knight was happy for the first time in many years. The happiness was short lived. The first person The Brave Knight came across spoke a language that the Brave Knight had never heard. His skin was a different color, too. The Brave Knight was completely confused. Then, he realized the very land itself had changed. When the land shook, Pangaea itself had changed. The seven continents were created. Each continent had different peoples with different languages. No one spoke the same language as the Brave Knight.

"The Brave Knight was now lost in a desert, a land with no food or water. He gave into temptation and ate a piece of the fruit of the Tree of Life. So, determined was he to live long enough to make it home. However, this act had made him immortal. It would take him many generations for him to finally find his way home. By then, his beloved Forever Queen was long gone.

"The Brave Knight had now become the Lonely Knight. He roamed the Earth still in love with his queen, forever separated from her by time and death. He had outlived every one he loved or even knew. His actions had caused great pain and heart breaks all over the world. You see, families had been separated by oceans and divided by languages. He realizes now that even though at the time, he thought he was doing the right thing in the name of love, he was really only thinking of himself. He was thinking only of what he wanted. He wanted the hand of the Forever Queen."

"Why are they called the Forever Queen and the Brave Knight? What were their real names?" Ilove asked.

"No one remembers. Their names were lost long ago with the sands of times." Trailynn explained. She then continued her story.

"One day, in deep despair, the Brave Knight cried out asking why he had been so forsaken to such a horrible existence, to wander the world all alone, unloved, for all time. He heard the two words whispered back to him on the wind…. *free will*"

"He understood in an instant. What can I do to end my suffering? I cannot die and I cannot continue to live this way. I am so alone. I am so unhappy. I am afraid to speak to anyone. I am afraid to care for anyone. I am afraid to love anyone. My heart can break no more. So, he became the man on the moon, to live out his immortality half way between heaven and earth. He watches over the world and shines his moonlight down wherever he can to help others, especially little girls that are lost in the dark or perhaps just need a little light to help them find their way home." Trailynn smiled at the conclusion of her story.

"Great story, but I thought they went to the moon and only found a big dusty rock?" Ilove yawned.

"Yeah, ain't that a shame. Science went and messed up a perfectly good story." Trailynn chided. "Get some sleep. I love you, Ilove. Good night."

"I love you, Mommy. That was a pretty great story."

Chapter Twenty Three

Ilove went to the woods every day after school. She would come home for dinner and share her escapades with her mother. One particularly bright and breezy day, Ilove asked her if she ever wanted come with her.

"Mommy, would you like to come to the woods with me? It's the prettiest day so far this week." Ilove ventured. "You can meet my animal friends."

Trailynn had been desperately wanting go with Ilove, but she didn't dare ask. She didn't want to intrude. She did, however, want to know what it was about the woods that made her daughter feel so at home. She wanted to understand her daughter better.

She also hoped to catch another glimpse of the fairies. This last part, she would never confess to aloud.

"Yes. I would really like that. I admit to being very curious about what you find appealing in those woods." Trailynn replied. She packed a snack and off they went.

"Hello, Mr. Bunny. This is my mother. Mrs. Kingston to you I guess." Ilove motioned to the rabbit slowly munching on a daisy. "Mommy, this is Mr. Bunny. He likes it when I find him clover under a shade tree for him to eat while I read." Ilove giggled, no way is she going to believe any of this.

"Nice to see you, have you seen any clover? This daisy is all right, but clover is better." Mr. Bunny said in between nibbles.

"He says it's nice to meet you. And you know full well the clover is over there." Ilove stated. "Go on over and I'll be there in a minute. I want to finish introducing my mother to the others. I've brought another book. This is a big one about a boy wizard."

Ilove looked up in the trees to see if she could find Mrs. Robin. Not seeing her, she then searched about with her eyes to see who all had come for story time today.

"Over there on that low branch, do you see those two dragonflies? The blue one is Azure and the green one is Clover. She prefers to go by Cloven though. I've never really asked her why. I think she just likes the sound of Cloven better."

"Hello! Glad you are here today. This is my mother, Mrs. Kingston!" Ilove called out to the fairies. "She has come to join us today!"

Trailynn had gotten her wish. She was seeing the fairies again. She just didn't know it.

"Oh my! Those are the prettiest dragonflies I have ever seen. They almost don't look real. They look more like crystal figurines." Trailynn marveled.

Ilove laughed a touch nervously, "That's just the magic of the light here."

The dragonflies appeared to bow their heads a bit in acknowledgement. Trailynn noticed the gesture, but thought to herself that she was making way too much out of their actions. No way that the dragonflies were aware of her.

"They say "thank you" and "welcome." Ilove said to explain their actions.

Nope. No way, Trailynn thought.

"Everyone, this is my mother, Mrs. Kingston. She's come for story time. I've brought a new book." Ilove walked over to her usual shady spot under the oak tree and settled down near Mr. Bunny. Trailynn stood awkwardly for a moment before realizing that she should also sit down. She selected a spot by Ilove, but made sure to give Ilove plenty of room.

Ilove pulled out a thick book.

"This is a big one, so it will take a while for us to read the whole book." Ilove began to read. Occasionally, she would reach over to ruffle Mr. Bunny's fur.

Trailynn watched her daughter, noticing how she reacted and interacted with all of the nature around her. She also began to notice as the audience continually grew. There were deer, raccoons, squirrels, a couple of foxes, and almost all of the lowest limbs were weighed down with birds of every color. All were focused on Ilove, captivated by her. Trailynn wondered how Ilove was doing this. The animals truly seemed to be listening to the story. "What a mystery my daughter is?" She thought.

The afternoon faded into evening and it was time to head back home. Ilove seemed to notice without Trailynn having to say a word.

"Okay, I'll be back tomorrow. How does everyone like the book so far?" Ilove announced. She looked around the crowd as if she were listening to them. "Oh! Good I'm glad I picked this one. Thank you all for being nice to my mom!"

During dinner, Trailynn seemed lost in her thoughts. She had seen much to think about.

"Are you all right, mommy?" Ilove perceived the silence as a problem.

"Yes, I'm fine. I am just thinking about today. I did see you today. I mean *really* saw you. The woods are where you belong. You seemed more as ease there surrounded by wild animals than at school or in town with other people. You also appeared to actually believe that you could have conversations with the animals. Is that really true? I've never heard of such a thing. I don't know how it can be possible. I considered that you might need a doctor or some sort of help, but after today. I just don't know what to think or do." Trailynn admitted all her concerns. "I know there are many things in this world that are unexplainable. I think I witnessed one today. I'm not sure what to do with that."

"I know that no one else has the same ability that I do. I *can* understand the animals. It's a gift." Ilove knew that she couldn't explain further. The fairy folk are secret. She promised to keep that secret. "I can't really explain it either. I've always been able to do it. I just go with it." Ilove paused before adding. "You are the only person I have trusted with that. No one else knows what I can do."

Trailynn just nodded as if she understood. Then, she wondered if Ilove's "gift" had anything to do with the fairies.

Chapter Twenty Four

The following Saturday Ilove could hardly wait to get to Westfairland. She wanted to tell both Queen Gemeenah and King Roland about her mother's visit to the woods. She felt the need to confess that she had once told her mother about the fairy folk. Now, that her mother seemed more open to Ilove's zest for the woods, maybe she would be more accepting of the fact that fairies were real. She remembered that it was all supposed to be a secret, but it is very challenging to keep her Saturday activities to herself. There had to be a way to bring the two worlds together.

Clover dropped Ilove in the center of the village. Ilove was immediately stunned what she saw. The people were moving! Slowly, not quite walking around yet, but they were moving nonetheless, some more than others, of course.

"Is it not fascinating?" Clover asked. "I have no idea what is going to happen next and it is wonderful. You are breaking the enchantment. You are one of us, or at least, a part of one of us. I am feeling emotions that I am not sure of. Everything is our world is changing. Everything is new." Clover struggled in expressing herself.

Ilove understood that she really belongs here, but she could never leave her mother. She had to convince Queen Gemeenah that she had to tell her mother.

"Where can I find Queen Gemeenah? I have some things I need to talk to her about." Ilove asked in a hushed voice, full of awe.

"She is either in her rooms or with King Roland. She has dearly missed his friendship and council." Clover responded.

Ilove went to see King Roland first. Maybe she would be lucky and have both monarchs there for her to speak to. Queen Gemeenah was talking to King Roland. He was looking at her, but not responding.

"Ahem, I'm sorry for interrupting. I'm glad that you are both here though. I have something I need to talk to you both about." Ilove said as she walking in, while placing her wooden daisy crown on her head. She keeps her crown at King Roland's and always tries to wear it when speaking to him. She could not think of a way to explain the crown to her mother without telling all. It was safer to leave it here and avoid the whole topic.

"It is all right. I was just catching King Roland up." Queen Gemeenah replied. "I have deeply missed my friend. Is something wrong?"

Ilove sat in a chair across from Queen Gemeenah. The tinkling sound of the bluebells let Ilove know that King Roland had also turned his head to listen. That is the biggest movement that she had witnessed. Amazement showed on her face.

A small laugh escaped from Queen Gemeenah, "It is wonderful, is it not?"

"It is. It is wonderful. I'm glad that I could help." Ilove said. "Maybe today he will regain his voice. My mother went to the woods with me the other day. She watched while I read to the animals. I introduced her to all and told her what they said in return. I'm not sure what she thinks about it all. I want to share with her about Westfairland. I think she is ready to believe me. I know that the existence of fairy folk and all other magical peoples are supposed to be secret, but I feel torn. She said she understands now that I do feel more at home in the woods. I think now I can explain why I feel that way."

"I see." Queen Gemeenah countered. "Is the secret causing you trouble?"

"Only within me. My mother has not asked or questioned me lately, but I feel the secret is really heavy between us. I know I can trust her with what is happening here. With all of you. She doesn't have many friends and even if she did say anything by accident, she would just say that it is my active imagination. She would not tell. No one would believe her if she did. She wouldn't risk it."

"Risk it? What do you mean? What is there for her to risk?" Queen Gemeenah asked.

"Risk? People, humans, are always thinking that anything different is wrong. Wrong must be fixed. If she told other people that she believed fairies were real, they would think she has gone crazy. They would think that I was not safe being with her. They would mean well but ruin all. My mother would not risk losing me." Ilove was proud of her explanation.

"I see." Queen Gemeenah said again. "Do you think she would believe you?"

"Honestly, I don't know. But if nothing else, I can share my adventures with her. I used to and she always thought it was make believe. I think she would think that again. I have missed talking to her. I think you can understand that?" Ilove nodded her head toward King Roland. Queen Gemeenah understood the gesture.

After a moment of thought, Queen Gemeenah sighed. She did understand because she had missed sharing her life experiences with King Roland.

"I agree. I do understand. Tell her what you need to. There is no proof. She may very well think you are making it up. I see no reason to go to the council about this considering that most likely she would tell no one. The secret will still be maintained even in the telling."

"Whew! I'm so glad you said that. I didn't want to betray your trust and I couldn't keep the secret from her. I was feeling torn. Is that the right word?" Ilove was clearly relieved.

"Right enough, little one." Queen Gemeenah smiled. "What have you got to share with King Roland today?"

"Well, I was going to tell about sharing the woods with my mother. She packed a snack for us and I was reading..."

The morning went by quickly with both Queen Gemeenah and King Roland listening to every word. Ilove also spoke about school and the weather. She included as many mundane details as she could remember.

Her prattling kept both monarchs entertained. Both had memories of Iadore in their minds. Both astonished by the complexity of life for a true descendant to be found after such a long wait.

Chapter Twenty Five

At dinner on the following Tuesday, Ilove decided to tell her mother everything. She had chickened out the day before. She gave herself pep talks all day to work up her courage. Telling herself over and over "You can do this!" Mom will understand.

"So Mom… you know how I tell you about my adventures in the woods? And how I can talk to animals and stuff?" Ilove tentatively asked.

"Yes, I remember. I always loved listening to those stories. You haven't told one in a while. Why is that?" Trailynn chose her words cautiously. In her head she was excitedly thinking "This is the moment. She's going to tell me about the fairies!" She struggled to stay calm.

"Well, I haven't told you any stories lately because I didn't think that you believed me." Ilove paused. "I swear it's all true and there is more that I want to tell you. I haven't because I don't know how to convince you that it's all real."

"I'm sorry if I made you feel that way, afraid to share things with me. But you have to admit it's not normal for a person to talk to animals and claim that they have full two way conversations." Trailynn offered.

Ilove nodded. She did know it wasn't normal and this was the problem.

"I know. Okay, here's where this is going to get complicated. I really miss telling you everything. This is the deal I wish to make. I will tell you and you can choose to believe what you want. I won't be mad if you do not believe a word. I will just feel better that I can share. Your side of the deal is that you will not get mad at *me* for believing these things. What do you think?" Ilove was kind of proud of herself. This was starting off better than she thought, if she agrees of course.

"Hmm. I think that is very reasonable." Trailynn smiled at her daughter. "Deal! Do we shake on it or are we good?"

"We're good!" Ilove laughed, relief emanating from her. "So where to begin? I really can understand animals. We really are friends. And there's more. There are magical peoples in the world. I am a descendant of fairy folk. I think it had to come from Daddy's side since you do not have any gifts. I also have fairy friends. It's supposed to be a secret because magical folks and humans have a bad history."

Here Ilove stopped to try to see how her mother was taking this news. Trailynn was sitting there listening and seemed deep in thought. She didn't know if she should continue or wait. Ilove chose to wait.

Trailynn looked up at Ilove and realized that she was looking for some sort of response. The bit about her late husband being a fairy descendant was absolutely news. She also marveled that Ilove has determined on her own that the "fairy whatever" was from her father and not her. She also understood so much more about her peculiar child.

Trailynn smiled with a slight, slow nod of her head.

"I'm taking all that in. I need just a moment here. That was a lot." Trailynn believed every word. What she was asking herself is whether or not she should confess that she had seen two fairies? "I want to say first and foremost that I actually do believe you. Or at least that you believe what you are saying." Then, she was irritated at herself because she realized that she failed to fully commit to letting Ilove know that she knew she was being honest. "What I mean is that I know you are telling me true. The mention of fairies caught me off guard a bit. Well, because I have a secret. I have seen them! I didn't trust myself to admit that I really did *see* fairies and that fairies are real!"

Ilove gasped. "You knew?!"

"No not really. I mean well here's what happened. I was hanging laundry and some movement caught my eye. I looked to see what it was, expecting it be a deer or something, and it was small bits of light that popped into two fairies that were picking flowers. The poof… back to small bits of light and they were gone. I was so shocked. I doubted my own eyes. Then I was consumed by guilt because you had tried to tell me that fairies were real and I didn't believe you. I'm sorry about that. Even after I had seen the two fairies, I was still uncertain, but I could no longer keep you from believing or interacting if what I saw or think I saw was real." Trailynn sighed. She was also appreciating the relief that she now felt.

Smiling, Trailynn added, "Wow! I feel so much lighter inside now that I have gotten that out!" She giggled a little because she knew that Ilove felt this same thing a few minutes ago.

"You should brace yourself then, because there's more!" Ilove laughed too.

"Oh, no! All right. Tell me everything!" Trailynn said. "More than fairies and you are part fairy. This will be good!"

"I have to first tell you a story of the history of the fairies and people that I hang out with, that I am a descendant of." Ilove told her mother everything... King Roland, his mean brother King Richard, Queen Gemeenah, Violet, Isadora, Iadore, Azure, Clover (how she likes to be called Cloven), Edward...

Trailynn noticed that Ilove blushed a bit when she spoke about Edward. She didn't interrupt. She listened to every word. Occasionally, she indicated that Ilove should take a bite of dinner or a drink of tea.

Afterwards, they hugged before bed and both slept peacefully. No more secrets and nothing more hidden. Joyous.

Chapter Twenty Six

This became their new routine. Every day after school, Ilove would go to the woods to spend time with the animals. Azure and Clover were there most days as well. Afterwards, dinnertime was a retelling of the day.

Weekends, Ilove would spend the majority of her time in Westfairland and continue to share her adventures with her mother. Dinner was absolutely Trailynn's favorite part of each day. She loved seeing her daughter so happy. Westfairland was almost completely restored. Of all the stories Ilove told, Trailynn especially enjoyed tales of King Roland. What a good man he must be? Ilove clearly adores him, she thought.

Ilove thrived in Westfairland! Every one there, human and fairy, seemed to click with her. There, she felt free to be herself and did not worry about fitting in because she knew that she did. Westfairland is where she belonged. The only thing missing was her mother.

"Tell me what your mother is up to today." King Roland asked Ilove as they were walking through one of the wildflower gardens. King Roland looked forward to these walks with Ilove. He would point to each flower as he told her all he knew about it, all he had learned from the fairies.

"I'm not sure. She doesn't have a job, but she is always busy. She tends to our house, laundry, gardening... all kinds of stuff. She always says she is exhausted. We eat dinner together every night. We tell each other about our days, but everything always looks the same to me. So I don't really know what she does all day or how she does it." Ilove realized as she explained that she had never given this subject much thought before. She blushed in shame.

"What is it?" King Roland noticed the change in Ilove's mood.

"I just realized that I tell my mother everything about myself and my day, but I haven't really asked her about hers. I always thought it was an even thing, but it isn't and now I feel kind of weird about it." Ilove stated.

"I believe that I am getting to know and understand your mother from all the stories that you have shared with me. You may be a little embarrassed by this self-revelation, but I would be willing to bet that your mother enjoys your conversations as much or even more than you do. She may not realize the value of all that she does. She may not think of her daily life as exciting, but tell her that I disagree. I imagine that running a home seamlessly takes a great deal of skill, especially if you are unaware of any struggles. That is a tremendous gift from parent to child." King Roland could not keep the admiration out of his voice. Trailynn must be quite a woman!

That night at dinner Ilove remained silent. She was determined to listen to whatever story her mother had to tell about her day.

"Did you have a bad day?" Trailynn asked. "You are unusually quiet. What happened today?"

"Today, I realized that I have been terribly selfish and I'm sorry." Ilove whispered.

"What?" Trailynn was completely unprepared for such a response. "I don't know what you mean."

"I mean. We agreed no more secrets and to share everything. I realized today when I was talking to King Roland that I tell you all about my day, but I'm so caught up in my own stuff that I have never really listened to you about your days. I'm sorry. I really want to hear about your day." Her voice was thick with emotion.

"And how did you come to think this?" Trailynn asked.

"King Roland asked me what you were doing while I was there and I didn't have an answer."

"I see. Did you just say that you didn't know or what did you say?" Trailynn was trying to see how this conversation went. How did this play out, she wondered.

"I told him that you didn't have a job but you were always busy. That our home always looked the same, so I didn't know what you did all day but you were always tired." Ilove said all this like she knows her answer will be an insult.

"And what did King Roland say? Does he think that I'm a lazy woman that does nothing all day?" Trailynn was hurt by the idea that King Roland would think this of her.

"He said that you must be a great mother to be able to take care of everything and make it seem easy. He said he thought that you were giving me a great gift but never letting me know if we are struggling or in need of anything." Ilove paused, sighed. "I think he is right. It always looks the same because you make sure everything is as it should be. We have food to eat. Clean clothes to wear. I don't even know if we are poor or have money. I think we are somewhere in the middle, but I don't really know." A small giggle escaped.

"We are not poor, but we are also not wealthy. Somewhere in the middle is a good way to say it." Trailynn was impressed by her daughter's thought process. King Roland had defended her! "I take care of all the things you mentioned. I do the washing, the cleaning, the cooking, and the gardening. I do all the gardening since you spend so much time away from home. There is nothing exciting about my day. I try to have everything done before you get home so that I can pay attention to your stories. Of the two of us, you are the adventurous, exciting one."

"I shouldn't take it for granted." Ilove murmured. "Thank you for all that you do, mom! I love you!"

Trailynn smiled. "I love you too! Do you feel better?"

"I do."

"Good. Then tell me about your day!" Trailynn eased back in her chair at the table, ready to enjoy her favorite part of the day.

Chapter Twenty Seven

Early one spring morning, Ilove was straightening her room when she found a doll with a fake leather jacket.

"Oh! I thought I lost you ages ago!" Ilove exclaimed to the doll. Then, she smiled at an idea she had for the jacket. She removed the jacket and cut two slits in the back. Her mother had taught her how to sew to make minor repairs. Carefully, she hemmed up the slits to prevent the lining from fraying. Pleased with her work, Ilove found a small box to wrap up her gift.

It was mid-morning by the time she got to the woods. Ilove hoped that Azure or Clover would be there still to take her to Westfairland. Luckily, her wish came true.

"Where have you been?!" Azure yelled.

"I'm sorry I'm late. Cloven, this is for you. We may have to make some adjustments for the right fit." Ilove said while handing Clover the small present.

"For me? I cannot imagine..." Clover murmured. "It is a very pretty box. Thank you."

"Open the box. Don't fairies wrap presents?" Ilove giggled.

"Oh, no. Normally, we just give the gift. What is the purpose of wrapping?" Azure explained a hint of hurt in her voice. She wondered why Ilove would give Clover a gift and not her.

"I don't know. I've never thought about a why. It's just what we do. Maybe it is to make sure it's a surprise?" Ilove was puzzled by the question. Why does the wrapping matter? It's what is inside that is important.

Clover opened the gift and gasped.

"I love it!" Clover held up the jacket, noticing the slits. She attempted to put it on. She had never worn human clothes before. Fairies naturally manifest their coverings naturally, gossamer coverings in their own unique color. Some fairies will add flowers and such. "Hmm. How does this work?"

Ilove helped Clover with the jacket, gently putting her wings through the slits as she shrugs the jacket onto her shoulders. Clover spun around with glee.

"How does it feel? Do the slits rub on your wings? We can make adjustments if we need to." Ilove wanted the jacket to be comfortable.

"I do not know how it is supposed to feel. I love it!" Clover cannot believe the thoughtfulness of the gift. "I feel like it fits me. Thank you! Thank you so much!"

"I'm sorry I don't have something for you Azure. I'm always on the lookout for things that I think you would like, both of you really. "Ilove says this to both of them, but really she is talking to Azure. She did not mean to hurt her feelings.

"I understand." Azure replies. "Are you ready to go?"

"Absolutely!"

Off they went. Amazingly, the jacket changed like Ilove's clothes. Ilove worried that Clover would not be able to wear the jacket while flying.

Upon arrival, Clover was beyond happy. She walked proudly through the village, showing off her new jacket, letting all know that it was a gift from her friend, Ilove. Azure could not watch the spectacle, leaving Ilove by King Roland's house.

King Roland was waiting for Ilove at the large table where he sat frozen for so many years. Ilove had to do a double take. For a moment, she feared that he was cursed again. Relief washed over her when he looked up to smile at her in greeting.

"Late start this morning?" he asked.

Ilove smiled back as relayed the events of her week and ended with the jacket for Clover.

"My goodness. That was a really considerate gesture." King Roland offered. "I don't know Clover very well, but from what I can tell about her that jacket is perfect for her." Then, he smiles as he got an idea of his own.

The following Saturday, King Roland gives Ilove a present for her mother.

"You have told me so much about her. I think she is so generous by letting you spend so much time here. I wanted to give something that would show her my appreciation for her sacrifice." King Roland said shyly. "I was inspired by you."

Chapter Twenty Eight

"Oh, I wonder what it could be. Imagine, me getting a gift from a King!" Trailynn was so delighted, opening the gift gently to preserve as much of its elegant wrapping as possible. Inside, she found a delicate intricately decorated bottle filled with some sort of liquid and a scroll tied with a lovely purple ribbon sealed by stamped red wax. "Wow!" was all the she could manage to say.

Carefully, she opened the scroll.

Dear Trailynn,

This is just a small gesture to show my appreciation of your sacrifice of Ilove's time. As a parent, I treasured each moment with my daughter, Iadore. She has been lost to me for many, many years. Ilove has restored my heart and brought life back to my kingdom. She is such an enchanting girl. She reminds me much of my Princess.

I am sending you a bottle of wildflower nectar. The fairies make this delicious drink that I very much enjoy with cookies most afternoons. I do hope that you too will enjoy the nectar. It has quite a unique taste.

Best Wishes,

King Roland the 20th of Westfairland

Something about the King's letter touched Trailynn's heart. He sounded lonely; even though she knew he was surrounded by people and loved ones. She understood completely. She too has a lonely heart since she lost her husband to a long forgotten war. She was proud of his sense of duty. She loved him dearly. Ilove was too young when he left to remember much about him.

Then she realized that King Roland was only partially right. Yes she was forgoing a lot of mother-daughter time with Ilove by letting her go with the fairies, but she was incredibly grateful because Ilove finally found a place where she belonged. With people, and fairies, that she connects with. She is so much happier now than she has ever been. As a mother, she could ask for nothing more.

She let out a gasp as she realized how much she wanted to share these thoughts with King Roland. The rest of the day, she spent going through her recipes. She wanted to return the gesture with just the right thing.

At first, she was going through all her cookie recipes, but thought what about a sweet cake or something that would show off her baking skills. He is a King after all.

She settled for a carrot cake, but then realized she didn't have enough carrots from the garden. Ilove came home from school to find her mother sitting at the table surrounded by all the recipes. She looked every bit as overwhelmed as she felt.

"Hi, Mom. Ah, what are you doing?" Ilove asked clearly, puzzled. She had never come home to her mother in such a state.

"I was looking for something to bake for King Roland. I settled on making a carrot cake, but I don't have enough carrots from the garden. He said that he likes cookies, but there are so many different kinds. I don't know what direction to take there. That's when I thought of the cake or sweet bread idea, but I've never made anything for a King. What if he doesn't like it or it's so bad he thinks of it as an act of war?" All this came out in one rushed breath.

Ilove giggled. Surprised her mother was so worked up.

"Relax. I got this." Ilove walked out to the garden where the carrots were planted. There were plenty of carrots, just all too small for what her mother needed. "You forgot why I go to Westfairland in the first place. I'm part fairy. Violet has been teaching me how to use my gifts. Watch this."

Ilove knelt down and held both of her hands out above the carrots. Closing her eyes to concentrate, she reached down inside herself. She found the energy from her fairy gift. The more she focused on the energy the stronger it grew. She heard her mother gasp and smiled. It was working. When she opened her eyes again, all the carrots were gigantic.

"Do you think you have enough carrots now?" Ilove couldn't take the pride out of her voice. She couldn't wait to tell Violet about this.

"You know I believed you about the being part fairy business before, but if there was any lingering doubt. Well, I certainly don't have any now. I guess we will never really go hungry." Trailynn laughed nervously. "Can you do other things?"

"Yes, but this is my best thing. I'm still learning all that I can do. Violet is a great teacher. I wish you could meet her." Ilove looked forward to the day that her two worlds would become one.

"So does this mean that you think the carrot cake is a good idea?" Trailynn asked. "You know the King. What does he like?"

"Honestly, mom, I think he will be thrilled with anything you make. Mainly, because you made it for him."

"What is that supposed to mean?" Trailynn replied a touch defensively.

"I mean, he is a really nice man and he appreciates everything others do. He knows that no one has to do anything for anyone else. So when somebody does something nice for him, it could be the worst dish ever made and he would still be thankful. As far as what he likes. I don't really know. I have seen him eat cookies, but I have never asked him what kind." Ilove hoped her mother would relax a little. It's just a gesture. Sheesh!

Chapter Twenty Nine

Trailynn in the end decided to make Ilove's favorite cookies for the King. She canned the carrots. She knew that Ilove could just grow more, but didn't see the sense in being wasteful. She found a cute little basket and lined it would some napkins she made using some of her wedding lace. It was the fanciest material she had. Carefully, she placed the slightly warm sugar cookies with butter cream icing into the basket. She arranged and rearranged the cookies.

The letter was a different ordeal all together.

After many, many false starts, she decided the best plan was to just write from her heart.

Dear King Roland,

You cannot imagine how strange this is for me to write. Never in a million years did I ever think I would be writing a personal letter to a King.

I am most likely breaking all kinds of protocol with what I am about to say, but I feel I must.

You are incorrect! (How often does a King hear that?)

Yes I do miss spending time with Ilove, but it is a worthy sacrifice. Plus, she tells me all about Westfairland. I feel as if I know many of you already even though we've not actually met.

Ilove has always been a peculiar child. She has never really fit in at school or in town. However, she does fit in with all of you. I have never seen her so happy. This is a best a mother can ask for her child. For this, I am truly, deeply grateful. I imagine that you understand this sentiment, as it is our daughters that we have in common.

I'm also incredibly grateful to you. My husband went to war one day when Ilove was very young. He was fully of pride. Sadly, he did not return to us. You, I feel, have filled that hole in Ilove's heart. She speaks so highly and fondly of you. I have no words for what this means to me. I sincerely thank you for being a part of my daughter's life.

I greatly enjoyed the wildflower nectar. I have no comparison for the taste. It gave me a warm glow inside, like I was drinking sunshine. I remembered you mentioned you enjoy the nectar with cookies. I wanted to repay the gesture. These are sugar cookies with butter cream frosting. Ilove's favorite. I hope you enjoy these as well. I'm a far cry from a royal baker. I hope these are acceptable.

Warmest wishes,

Trailynn Kingston

She folded and tucked the letter in with the cookies.

Chapter Thirty

The letters and small gifts continued to be sent by both King Roland and Trailynn. Ilove was always puzzled by the excitement and the delight her mother showed with each of her deliveries. She watched as her mother poured over King Roland's letters. She appeared to be savoring each and every word. She would cherish the gifts, some were as simple as lily or a rose. Trailynn would press each flower she received to preserve the flower so that she could treasure it.

"It's just a flower, Mom. They grow everywhere." Ilove would say, clearly missing the significance her mother saw. Her mother would blush and smile in response, deepening Ilove's confusion.

"I don't know why my mother gets so excited about the flowers and other things you send her. I pick flowers for her all the time and she doesn't get all googly about it." Ilove complained to King Roland. The two had taken to walking together through Westfairland instead of the King's house.

Amused, King Roland said, "I believe I would very much like to meet your mother. I have also grown quite fond of her letters and small tokens."

"Really? She doesn't have any fairy blood. Is that even possible?" Ilove was truly puzzled now.

"I do not see why not. I, nor any of my people, have fairy blood and we are here." King Roland realized that he had not even thought about the possibilities of actually meeting Trailynn. Her letters and gifts were often the highlight of his days. He was still musing over the hazelnut banana bread he received yesterday. He had never tasted anything like it before. He joked to himself that it was his new favorite treat, but knew the bread would most likely be replaced with the next letter.

He became aware that Ilove was staring at him. He was lost in his thoughts of Trailynn, a woman he only knew by words on a pages and stories from her daughter. He wondered if he was getting a true impression of her in his heart.

"I am sorry. I got lost in my thoughts for a moment. Please, do not mention the possibility of bringing your lovely mother for a visit. I will require a bit of time to consult with Queen Gemeenah. We rule together and I cannot make decisions rashly." King Roland explained. "So tell me, how are you doing with your lessons? At home and here with Violet?"

Ilove began to tell him all about school and stated her very obvious dislike for math. King Roland was only half listening. His mind was preoccupied with thoughts of Trailynn. What is she like? Is she really as beautiful as Ilove describes her? Does she want to meet him too? Would she like Westfairland? I mean we live in a big cave. It is a different way of life than what she is used to. Maybe she would hate it and not return. Or maybe she would consider living here with Ilove. Should he find a place for them to stay? Would she want her own house or would she want to stay with one of the villagers?

King Roland chuckled to himself. He understood that he was getting way ahead of himself. Queen Gemeenah would have to give her blessing before any of these questions were even relevant.

Ilove heard his small laughter. She didn't think she had said anything funny, but decided that it must be an adult thing. Adults always seemed to think that kids were amusing. She just kept babbling. He seemed to be hanging on every word.

Chapter Thirty One

"Queen Gemeenah may I have a word?" King Roland approached her on the little bridge that crossed the rivulet that meandered roughly through the center of the cavern.

"Of course. Let us go to my place as you humans like to say."

Queen Gemeenah had been happier than she had been in decades. All the humans were free of the Unmoving curse. Daily life of yesteryear had been restored. "I, too, have some things that I wish to discuss with you. I also have a fresh bottle of wildflower nectar to share. How does that sound?"

"Marvelous!" King Roland had sent the last of his bottle of wildflower nectar to Trailynn. He was not sure how Queen Gemeenah would feel about that, so he opted not to mention it. In a flash, they two monarchs were flying through the air as a small ball of light. Even after all these years, King Roland was still not quite used to this mode of transport.

Queen Gemeenah served King Roland a flower cup of wildflower nectar and offered some honeyberry cakes. King Roland had settled on one of the lounging cushions to gather his thoughts.

"I think it is time to plan a festival." Queen Gemeenah blurted out before King Roland could say a word. "A new festival. A new tradition. We need to celebrate finding Ilove and the end of the Unmoving curse. We can invite others to join us. I am sure King Minegard would come and I thought we could extend an invitation to the witches. While we are at, why not just include everyone we can think of?" Queen Gemeenah was vibrant with excitement.

"Would "everyone" possibly include Ilove's mother?" King Roland ventured. He was so nervous about how to bring up the idea of Trailynn coming to Westfairland and Queen Gemeenah presented the perfect opportunity.

"Ilove's mother?" Queen Gemeenah had not clearly expected the question. Her mood instantly changed. "Another human? I suppose she does know of us." She paused. "I had to consult with the Magical Folk Counsel to allow you to stay. Would that approval extend to Ilove's mother since Ilove is a descendant and part fairy? Oh, things to consider." Another pause. "Tell me, why do you think we should include her and do you think that she will come?"

"I would imagine Trailynn is most curious about Westfairland and the peoples that live here. Ilove is here as much as she home. Wouldn't you be curious about who your only daughter is spending so much time with?" King Roland thought that he would get out of having to omit his own desire to meet Trailynn. Avoid admitting that she has captured his imagination and possibly a place in his heart. He felt silly for having feelings for someone he did not know, but he did know her. He believed he had gotten to know her very well through her letters.

"Yes. I would indeed, but I sense there is more." Queen Gemeenah knew about the letters that were being exchanged. She did not know the content of course. "Could the invitation have anything to do with letters the two of you are exchanging?"

King Roland blushed deeply. He should have known she knew about their correspondence. Very little escaped her.

"Maybe a little." He whispered. He was too shy and a slightly embarrassed to be called out so blatantly.

"Very well." Queen Gemeenah was charmed by King Roland's behavior in regard to Trailynn. Those must be some letters she thought to herself with a giggle. "The invitation will come from me. While I am thinking, I think you should send the invitations to the Magical peoples and I will invite the humans. How does that sound?"

"I suppose that would work, but..." King Roland paused. How does he confess that he wanted to personally invite Trailynn. He had already been working out what he wanted to say to her in the invite. And why was Queen Gemeenah taking this position. "I was kind of wanting to invite her myself. Like a personal invite from me to her." His face was red from embarrassment.

"Yes I am sure you do. However, you have been exchanging communications for a long time now. However, I believe it is time for me to introduce myself. I also think it would be very well received by the magical peoples to receive an invitation from a human. Do you think that Trailynn would decline the invitation if it came from me instead of you?" Queen Gemeenah's words were weighted with hidden humor. She was enjoying his discomfort a little. Why would he not just admit that he was curious about Trailynn and wanted to get to know her personally? Perhaps he even believes he has genuine emotions for her? "Yes. I believe this should be our course. What did you want to discuss?"

"Oh!" King Roland was once again disarmed by the Queen. "I was thinking the same thing oddly. It is time for a celebration. I was thinking about the old festivals that we enjoyed and thought it is time to have another. I did not go so far as to think of an entirely new event." King Roland hoped that his words were believable. It wasn't a complete lie. "I will work on the invite. I have not had an opportunity to address magical folks. I will get your advice when I get my thoughts together. I would not wish to offend any group from my lack of knowledge or experience."

Secretly he hoped that Queen Gemeenah would make the same offer, but she intentionally made no offer.

Chapter Thirty Two

All of Westfairland came alive with activity in preparation for the festival. The entirety of the cavern was filled fresh aromas and noise from all the commotion... breads being baked, new flowers growing, benches were being made, etc. Everywhere you looked fairies and humans were busy. All to the detriment of King Roland.

King Roland sat at his table with wads of crumpled up rejected invitations surrounding him. He found something lacking with each draft he wrote. He was convinced that each offended one group or another. This just added to his misery. At least this is what he told himself. The truth is that he was in agony over Queen Gemeenah's invitation to Trailynn. He knew that the Queen would be respectful and kind, welcoming even, but what would she say about him? Would he even be mentioned? If so, by who? Queen Gemeenah or Trailynn?

Now that he was thinking about this, what has Ilove told her mother about him? Would she disappointed when whatever craziness Ilove had told her turned out to be untrue? Oh! The sweet torture of the unknown!

King Roland also had to question himself over the depths of his feelings for Trailynn. Her letters and gifts were his treasures and delights. His realized that his heart had not moved like this since his beloved Isadora. What if everything he felt and thought turned out to be false. What if it was all true and these feelings were only one sided? Or best possibility, all true and mutual? What if she declined the invitation? But why would she? She has to be as curious about him as he was about her.

All this will be over soon enough. He needed to find a way to concentrate on the invitations that he agreed to send. He paused a moment before resuming the task and instead, decided it was time to consult with Queen Gemeenah.

Queen Gemeenah found Ilove helping Edward make benches. Before interrupting to speak to Ilove, she noticed the wonderful way the two half fairies got along. They joked and laughed together as if they had known each other all their lives. She also took note of Ilove wearing the lovely crown that Edward had made for her. "Hmm..." Queen Gemeenah thought to herself.

"Ilove, may I have a word?" Queen Gemeenah asked.

"Of course!" Ilove always looked forward to talking to the Queen.

"Before you leave today with Azure and Clover, will you come find me? I wish to go to your home with you." Said Queen Gemeenah.

"Ah, okay. Uh, no problem." Ilove was suddenly nervous over the Queen's request. Ilove's mind raced for explanations. Had she done something wrong?

Evidently, Ilove confusion and concern was plainly visible on her face.

Queen Gemeenah chuckled, "Have no fear. I merely wish to invite your mother to the festival. I wish to do so in person. Is that all right?"

"Absolutely! I know she would love to meet you." Relief washed over Ilove's face. "I never thought about my mother coming here. She says she feels like she knows all of you from all the stories I've told her. Nothing bad, of course."

"I can see how she would believe so. I will let you get back to Edward. I mean, the benches." Queen Gemeenah said with a knowing look that made Ilove blush ever so slightly.

King Roland met Queen Gemeenah by the bridge that crossed the small rivulet that divided Westfairland.

"Hello, my friend. I hope we are well met!" Queen Gemeenah called out.

"Indeed we are!" King Roland paused. "Though I did come to find you. I am having a bit of difficulty with the invitations. I feel that each attempt I have made I offend some one. For example, I tried to go with friendly and informal at first. It is a festival not royal ball. Then I tossed that idea out because I thought it too informal and presumptuous. As in assuming we are friends when many I have not met. I wrote one missive stating that it was just a short notes and immediately thought the dwarves would take offense and refuse to come. You see why I am struggling? I also do not know how to say the day of the festival. For us, we said in a week's time, but we use gemlight to track our days and nights. What do other magical peoples use to keep track? Is daylight the same? And do they all read and understand English? Do I need to specify each…?"

Queen Gemeenah disrupted King Roland's ramblings with a giggle.

"What is so amusing?" King Roland demanded. "I am having real troubles here!"

"My apologies!" Queen Gemeenah went from a small giggle to a full on belly laugh. "I mean no offense. I knew that you would face such issues and I thought it comical. I did not intend such hardship. Please, come with me and I will show you how it is done."

In a flash, Queen Gemeenah and King Roland were lighting to her chambers.

King Roland sat down immediately.

"Still not used to traveling by light even after all these years?" Queen Gemeenah asked.

"Not even close." King Roland replied, gesturing to a jug of wildflower nectar on her table, "May I? It always seems to help."

"Of course! Help yourself!" Queen Gemeenah called over her shoulder. "Let me know when you have settled enough to continue."

King Roland took a few sips of nectar and of moment of rest before saying he was ready to continue. "Okay. Show me what you got! I mean show me how to get the invitations out without being rude or offensive."

"Honestly, I knew you would have trouble, but I did not anticipate this much. I thought you would ask me from the start. My apologies. I also know that you would prefer to personally invite Ilove's mother. I am aware of your communications. I just believe I need to have a word before bringing her. All things considered."

"You do not think that she will tell other humans, do you?" King Roland asked astonished.

"Oh, no! I just feel that due to my commitments to the other magical leaders and all the rules regarding humans, it is just better to be wise and cautious. This would be my way of making sure I do not offend." Queen Gemeenah explained with a wink. "As with all things, we live and work with nature."

Queen Gemeenah gestured to a wall of yellow trumpet flowers that were mixed with a strange flower that he had never seen before. Those flowers were of every color he could imagine. Such a beautiful sight. Then, he noticed that those flowers appeared to be moving. Oh! They were not flowers at all! They were hundreds of small butterflies!

"We use the trumpet flowers to carry messages to our neighboring magical communities and the butterflies for those a bit farther away. Rarely, do we need to send any messages very long distances, but on the occasion where that is required, we use a song bird to carry our missives on the wind."

"Marvelous!" King Roland could not contain his amazement.

"To answer one of your other questions, yes gemlight and daylight are pretty close to the same. The only difference is the time of awakening and sleep. Gemlight is set and daylight, of course, is based on sun movements. Gemlight is set in roughly 4 sessions. Awakening is when the gemlight starts to shine. The gemlight slowly brightens to simulate sunlight that our crops can grow by. Then, just as slowly, the gemlight begins to fade into the fourth and final phases which consider night. As you know, we do not have an actual sun or moon. We use various gems to simulate the times of day and night. Citrines for sun and diamonds for stars. I am sure you have noticed the opal moon. All of our gemlight phases and times are in tune with nature. That is what makes the days roughly the same here as other parts of the world." Queen Gemeenah paused to make sure King Roland is following along. He nodded and she continued.

"I believe we set the festival for a week from Saturday?" she turned to see King Roland nod again.

Queen Gemeenah turned to the flowered wall to issue the invitations.

"To All Peoples Who Wish to Attend,

Queen Gemeenah and King Roland of Westfairland cordially invite you all to a celebration festival a week from Saturday."

With the clap of her hands, the wall became a flutter of movement. All the colorful butterflies took flight up through the top of her chamber to deliver the message.

"There that should do it." Queen Gemeenah said. After which, she turned to see a very unhappy King Roland. "What? Oh, I know. There is no way you could have done this and I did know it. As I said, I had no idea that you would struggle so. It was meant as a gaffe. I am truly sorry for the distress I caused you. Please, forgive me."

"Yes. I suppose I will *eventually* see the humor in this situation. In the meantime, I need to clean up the mess I made in my fruitless efforts." King Roland was only slightly aggravated. He had to keep in mind that if the roles were reversed there is a very good chance he would have done the same thinking it funny. After a moment, he chuckled. "You do realize I will have to think of some sort of payback for this."

"I do." Queen Gemeenah was relieved that King Roland was not terribly angry with her. Fortunately, his good nature had won out.

Both burst into giggles.

Chapter Thirty Three

Ilove waited with Clover while Azure went to let Queen Gemeenah know that she was ready to go home for the day.

"Why do you suppose Queen Gemeenah wants to meet my mother?" Ilove asked Clover.

"I do know. I am sure it is nothing to be concerned about. You have been coming here for quite a while now. Perhaps, Queen Gemeenah just simply thinks it is time to meet." Clover replied, shrugging on her jacket. The jacket Ilove had given her, sometimes it bothered her when she flew by light. Clover had the jacket enchanted to change sizes accordingly, but this was a foreign material and then enchantment did not quite work as effectively as it should. And she did not care. The black pleather jacket suited her and she loved it.

"Yes, I'm sure you are right." Ilove said reservedly.

Ilove watched as two small beautiful balls of light, one bright white with traces of color and one a vibrant blue, came down from the top cavern. The sight made Ilove smile.

"I don't think I will ever get tired of seeing fairies as light. It rocks my brain to think that I also turn into light when we fly together. It's just too much." Ilove said.

"What is too much?" Queen Gemeenah asked as soon as she alighted next to Ilove.

"Light travel. It's a thing. I mean no one, human I mean, would be able to imagine it and I actually get to do it." Ilove explained. "I know it's nothing to you, but for me, well, it's a bit hard on the brain." After a moment, Ilove added, "Don't get me wrong, I love it! Just can't think about the details, ya know?"

"I believe I do." Queen Gemeenah smiled. "Are we ready?"

The four of them stopped at the edge of the woods by Ilove's house. Ilove noticed that Queen Gemeenah had changed her appearance. She appeared to be wearing a gorgeous flowing gown made of the finest gossamer ivory colored silk with soft pastels and a crown of flowers. Ilove took a closer look at the crown, realizing that all the flowers and leaves on the dress and the crown were made of little jewels. Ilove immediately bowed to Queen Gemeenah out of instinct. There was no denying her majesty.

"This is how I appear for formal royal engagements." Queen Gemeenah stated. "I must make a proper first impression."

"Mission accomplished." Ilove blushed.

Ilove led the way to her house. Upon entering, she called out for her mother.

"I'm in the kitchen." Trailynn called.

"Uh, we have some company." Ilove managed.

Trailynn came into the living room, drying her hands on a dishtowel. Stunned and speechless by the fact that there were fairies staring at her. Self-consciously, she threw the towel back into the kitchen.

"Mom, I would like for you to meet Queen Gemeenah, Azure, and Cloven." Ilove pointed to each fairy in turn.

Trailynn nodded and then curtsied to Queen Gemeenah. After an awkward pause, she mumbled, "Your Majesty."

"Hello. I am pleased to meet you. As Ilove has stated, I am Queen Gemeenah of Westfairland. I have come to personally invite you to a celebration festival in kingdom. I co-rule Westfairland with King Roland. I understand that you are familiar with him?"

Trailynn nodded and curtsied again.

"Please, stop doing that. I understand why you feel the need to, but it is really not necessary. I sincerely hope that we become friends." Queen Gemeenah said.

"Yes, Your Majesty." Trailynn responded before catching in the middle of yet another awkward curtsey.

Queen Gemeenah laughed musically. "Really? Is my appearance that alarming?"

Trailynn relaxed just a touch. Finding her voice, "Well, to be honest, I have never been in the presence of a Queen before. Plus, there is the whole fairy thing. As in fairies, in my home. Here. Now." She added, "You could have told me they were coming! Some sort of heads up!" The fierce look on her face as she looked at Ilove caused Ilove shrink back a little.

"I didn't know!" Ilove exclaimed defensively. "She just asked me today!"

"Oh! No!" Queen Gemeenah said loudly. "I did not intended to cause a discord. Ilove is correct, I did only mention my desire to meet with you earlier today. I was not aware of the protocol. We shall leave and I will send a formal request. Is that the correct action?"

Trailynn was embarrassed by her own behavior.

"No. I apologize. To all of you." Trailynn blushed before continuing. "Yes I am aware of all of you. Ilove tells me of her visits to your kingdom every evening as we eat dinner or before bed. Even though I believe all that she tells me, I still had trouble actually accepting the knowledge, I think. Of course, you are welcome here. I was just caught off guard. Please, forgive my rudeness. Will you have a seat? Would you like something to eat or drink? I have some wildflower nectar that King Roland sent me. I must say that I understand why he enjoys it so." Trailynn gestured to living room. "Please."

Azure and Clover sat down, fascinated by everything in the human world. Queen Gemeenah remained standing.

"So, there is no need for a formal request?" Queen Gemeenah questioned. She was not entirely sure she understood what was happening.

"No, of course not. I reacted badly because, well, this is obviously not a normal situation. I'm just an ordinary person living an ordinary life. Having fairies in my home is a bit jarring. Having a Queen in my house is unimaginable. I just needed a moment to adjust. I'm embarrassed by my initial reaction."

"I believe I understand." Queen Gemeenah replied. "I must also apologize. I did not realize how our sudden appearance would affect you. I knew Ilove made you aware of our people. I imagined this going much more smoothly."

"She did and continues to tell me all about all of you. I just thought that this was her reality and not mine. I did not ever think that I would be included. I am grateful for all that you have done for Ilove. She is so much happier now than she has ever been. I believe it is due to her knowledge of her ancestry. I thank you for all that you have given her." Trailynn was visibly relaxing. Amazed by her own ability to adjust to such a surreal situation.

"Actually, it is we who are grateful and in great debt to Ilove. She has restored our kingdom. For that, we will be forever grateful." Queen Gemeenah bowed slightly to Ilove.

Ilove glowed at the praise. "Hey, want to come see my room?" she asked turning to Azure and Clover, who readily agreed, leaving Queen Gemeenah and Trailynn alone to speak more freely.

"Those three have grown very close." Queen Gemeenah advised Trailynn.

"So it seems. Funny, though, I believe Ilove has a doll that has a jacket just like... I'm sorry...what is the name of the green one again?"

"Clover, but she prefers Cloven. I confess that I do not completely understand why?" Queen Gemeenah answered.

"Youth, I would say. It is always a trial of self-discovery. The hard path we all must take to find out who and what we are." Trailynn offered as a possible explanation. "For those of us that have already been through the process, it can be terrifying and rewarding at the same time I think."

Queen Gemeenah looked at her intently. Almost as if really seeing her for the first time. She slowly began to nod her head. Trailynn did not know if the gesture was to demonstrate agreement or if the Queen had come to some sort of decision or conclusion.

After an awkward moment, Queen Gemeenah spoke.

"I would very much like for you to attend the festival. If you accept my invitation, I will arrange for someone to bring you to my kingdom. I do not believe the young ones will be quite strong enough. I would like to say that I would do so myself, but duty takes precedent. I do so hope that you understand."

Trailynn blushed. She struggled to imagine how she became a person that would host a queen in her home, have a king for a pen pal, and a daughter that is a half fairy. The unpredictably of life is astounding.

"I am honored to be invited, your Majesty. I would very much enjoy going to your kingdom. To be able to see all the things that Ilove has been telling and meet all the people. I am so flattered and humbled by all of this. I thank you sincerely for the invitation and gladly accept." Trailynn curtsied slightly.

Queen Gemeenah chuckled softly. She was thoroughly charmed by her.

"I regret having to mention this last bit, but I have many others to consider. I must stress the importance of secrecy. Though I welcome you to Westfairland, I am afraid the "adventure" must remain a secret. The magical community has very strict rules regarding humans and knowledge of peoples."

"Of course! Ilove explained the secrecy bit to me. To honest, I have no one to tell and if I did no one would believe me. Ah, did you say peoples? As in other magical races?"

Queen Gemeenah chucked again. It is a light, almost musical sound.

"Oh my dear, you have so much to learn!" With that, Queen Gemeenah called out to girls that it was time to go.

Chapter Thirty Four

The day of the festival arrived. The entire cavern was an explosion of color. Flowers, garlands, lights of every color covered almost every surface. The bakers had made a plethora of pies, breads, tarts, jellies, jams, all sorts of sweets. Wondrous food creations were every the eye could see. By the looks of the preparations, it was clear that every Westfairlandian (fairy and human) looked forward to the celebration. All the fruit trees were heavy with ripe delicious fruit. All was in readiness. It was to be the festival to beat all festivals!

Queen Gemeenah stayed behind to make sure that she was there with King Roland to greet each of the invited guests. She requested that Violet go with Azure and Clover to bring Trailynn and Ilove to the celebration.

Trailynn must have gone through every article of clothing she owned. She wasn't even this nervous on her wedding day! She wanted to look just right. She wanted to make sure that she didn't disappoint any of the Ilove's friends, especially King Roland. She had not heard from him in over a week. She worried about how or if she had offended him.

At long last, she had chosen a sun yellow dress with a white lace trim. She had been baking cookies for days to take to the festival. "Never show up empty handed!" She could hear her mother's words in her head. She made six dozen chocolate chip cookies and six dozen butterscotch with vanilla icing. She had no idea how many to people lived in Westfairland. A dozen dozen will have to do!

A gentle knock on the door interrupted Trailynn's thoughts.

"Coming!" Trailynn called. It's time! Nervously, she opened the door to the most resplendent purple fairy! The very sight of her made her speechless.

"Hello. My name is Violet. Queen Gemeenah sent me to bring you to Westfairland." Violet was not sure what to make of the expression on Trailynn's face. "For the festival? It is today." "Ah…yes…um…" Trailynn stammered. Then she gave herself a bit of a shake. "My apologies. I knew fairies were coming today to bring me to the festival, but honestly, it's still a bit of a jolt actually seeing you. You are purple and have wings and well, not a sight I ever believed I would see at my door. I'm afraid I will need a moment for my mind to play a catch up to reality. Please come in! A thousand apologies for my rudeness!"

Violet smiled softly as she stepped through the door.

"Thank you. I believe I understand. The magical peoples have remained hidden from the human world for many centuries. May I say what a lovely home you have?" Violet too was uncomfortable. Ilove is the only outside human that she had met. She did not know what to expect. All the stories tell of the horrors of humans. Edward and Ilove are part fairy. She wondered how a full human would behave.

"I made some treats to take to the festival. I'm packing them up now in baskets. Can we, you and I, carry these as we fly? Or light travel? Ilove tried to explain this to me, but I do not fully understand what that means. You know, this being my first fairy flight and all." Trailynn giggled nervously. *I'm making a fool of myself! Get a grip!* She thought to herself.

Violet looked around seeing the many baskets Trailynn had filled. There were six with two dozen cookies in each. Gently, she touched a glowing white stone on her necklace.

"I will require four." Violet said aloud.

Trailynn stared at Violet with her mouth slightly open. She appeared to be in the middle of asking something, but the words were stuck in her throat. That was not far off from the truth.

"This necklace is a way of speaking to my people in Westfairland. Azure and Clover are outside. They can each carry a basket. I have requested four more to carry the remaining baskets. I shall carry you. Ilove is already there. The young ones brought her over this morning." Violet spoke slowly.

"I see." Trailynn whispered. "Do I look all right? I have met your Queen once before, but I have never met a king. Is this good? Should I change? I don't have anything fancier, I'm afraid." She said after finding her voice. "Do you know him well?"

Violet also knew about the correspondences between King Roland and Trailynn. She smiled in remembrance of a similar conversation she had with him just before leaving the cavern.

"You look lovely and I am certain King Roland will be most pleased." Violet struggled to suppress a knowing giggle.

Another knock at the door ended the conversation before Trailynn could ask more about King Roland.

Opening the door, Trailynn gasped. Her eyes wide. Six fairies stood on the small porch. *I'll never get used to seeing them*, she thought.

"Trailynn allow me introduce you. Everyone this is Trailynn. She is Ilove's mother. Trailynn, this is Crimson, Marigold, Lilac, Peony, and of course, you already know the young ones Azure and Clover." Violet pointed to each fairy in turn.

"It is Cloven and you know it!" Clover huffed. "Are you ready?"

"Yes. I guess I am. I am curious. Are all fairies so stunningly beautiful?" Trailynn had an image in her mind of all the fairies that must fill Westfairland. What an awe-inspiring vision! "Please, come in. Here are baskets that I wish to take to the festival."

None of the fairies knew how to answer her question about the beauty of fairies. They all just quietly stepped into the house. Violet handed each a basket of cookies.

"What are these?" Crimson asked. His brow was furrowed with curiosity.

"Cookies? They are a sweet treat for dessert or a snack. Are cookies not a thing where you are from?" Trailynn said in a rush on the edge of panic. Did she make something that they couldn't eat?

"Hmm. May I?" Marigold asked.

"Of course! Please, help yourself! These are chocolate chip and those are butterscotch." Trailynn watched anxiously as each of the fairies selected a cookie to taste. She watched as they looked at each other holding a cookie, all questioning the other with their expressions as if to ask each other who would be the bravest and go first.

Clover took a small bite. She had selected a chocolate chip cookie while Azure held a butterscotch cookie. All eyes were on her.

"Mmmm!!! What are these little dark bits? They are delicious! I have not tasted anything like it!" She exclaimed as she took a much bigger bite.

Trailynn giggled. "That is chocolate."

After seeing Clover's reaction to the cookie, the rest of the group tasted of theirs. Trailynn laughed when Crimson licked the frosting on his cookie.

Looking at her, Trailynn said "That is vanilla frosting. I'm very glad that you all seem to like my cookies."

"Very much!" Marigold said. There were nods all around.

"Shall we go?" Violet asked after finishing her butterscotch cookie. She was answered with more nods as each grabbed a basket and headed out. Violet turned to Trailynn, "Ready?"

Trailynn nodded. "What do I do?" she asked as she closed the door behind them.

"Just take my hand. I will do the rest." Violet held out her hand to Trailynn.

Chapter Thirty Five

Trailynn had no words for the sensations she felt while flying. She gripped Violet's hand, and, in a whoosh, she was weightlessly soaring. She could see the ground going by beneath her. She could feel the wind against her skin, but at the same time, she couldn't feel her toes. She was flying! Her fear became joy. Glee! Pure glee!

She realized that they were deep in the woods that surrounded her cottage. This disorientated her a bit. She couldn't get a sense of the direction they were flying in. Before long, Trailynn noticed light coming from the edge of the forest. Almost, there she thought to herself.

Suddenly, the trees were gone and she was flying over the greenest valley imaginable. How could this beautiful place be so close to where she had lived her entire life and not known it was there? She glanced up to see the mountains.

"Ah," she thought, "the cave of Westfairland must be somewhere close by. I wonder how far we have travelled."

At the base of the highest mountain Violet rose up slightly. About halfway up the mountain, Trailynn noticed a black dot. The dot grew in size as they neared. She was seized by terror! There is no way I can go down that impossibly deep dark hole! Surrounded by all that rock! What if it collapses? Sure, the fairies can fly through it... they can be light, but she is human. What if the rules are different for her? What if she gets lost or trapped?

Her terror turned into a full-blown panic attack. Violet begin to struggle keep Trailynn in her grasp. She tried to reassure her that everything was all right, but Trailynn couldn't hear her or anything other than the thunderous beating of her heart.

Violet flew as fast as she could. She spotted a small landing outside the cave entrance and she aimed for straight for it. She realized that she needed to get Trailynn down on firm ground for her to catch her breath. This must be an overwhelming experience for a human she thought. She just needs a moment to collect herself.

"There, you are all right. See? Take a moment to catch your breath before we proceed. It is not much farther. Just a bit through the tunnel." Violet explained using the most soothing tone she could.

Trailynn was crumbled on the landing, clutching to the side of the mountain. She was frozen in place by fear. She just knew that if she let go of the rock face, she would fall to her death. Why had she ever thought she could do this?

"I can't. I can't move. I can't go on. I can't go soaring through a dark tunnel. I will never survive." Trailynn panted.

"Of course, you can. You can do all of those things. There is nothing to fear. I will fly slowly for you if the speed is the problem." Violet offered, stroking Trailynn's hair. "Ilove does this almost every day without any injury. I promise to take much care."

Trailynn acknowledged that Ilove did in fact make this journey practically every day without incident, but she was part fairy. What if it was different for her?

Then, her heart sank even further. She realized that if she didn't find the courage to face the darkness, she would never meet King Roland. If she was honest with herself that was not something she could live with. She could not go back to her home without seeing the man that had captured her imagination and heart with his words.

"Can we walk to Westfairland from here? Walk through the tunnel I mean? Would you walk with me? Light the way a bit. I'm sorry, but I cannot fly into that hole. The darkness is too great and we were going too fast…. Well, I just can't!" Trailynn was picturing a fly hitting a window at full speed. "I'm sorry…" Trailynn dissolved into tears, her body heaving with gut wrenching sobs.

Violet was at a loss. She did not expect this reaction. Humans are so odd, she thought.

"It will be all right." Violet offered. "I will go with you and soon you will see that there is nothing to fear." She extended a hand for Trailynn to help her get back up on her feet.

Tentatively, Trailynn took the offered help. Facing the tunnel entrance, she took a deep, shaky breath to steel her nerves. With an almost imperceptible nod, the two women took a small step forward.

"There." Violet said. "Even mighty rivers begin with a single tiny drop." She told the others in the group to go ahead to let the others know that they would be there shortly. "Shall we continue? You have already completed the hardest part."

"How so?" Trailynn asked. "I have only stood up and taken a small step." Her voice thick with questioning disbelief.

"You mustered your courage to face that which frightens you, yes?" Violet acknowledged Trailynn's nod, then continued. "What could possibly be harder than that?"

Trailynn could not help herself. She returned Violet's smile. Again, she gave a slight nod and took another step. She began to relax, telling herself that Violet was right and there was nothing to be afraid of. This worked for a while, but eventually the darkness of the passageway started to overwhelm her once more. Violet's fairy light was not nearly bright enough.

Violet was at a loss at to what to do. She is only a half light. Perhaps, she should go home to get another fairy to escort her. More light would certainly help. Violet had forgotten that she could have used the necklace charm.

"I am going home to get others to help. I am a half light. More fairies will mean more light. Please, sit and rest while I go." Violet gushed these words out before Trailynn could protest the plan.

Alone in the utter darkness, Trailynn felt small and unable to breath. The tears came in a torrent. First out of fear and then out of anger. She felt a deep disappoint in herself. Disappointed in her lack of courage. Disappointed that she failed King Roland.

"NO!!!" She yelled at herself. "I will NOT fail him!" Trailynn stood with a renewed fierceness. With her arms out stretched, she slowly headed in the direction she saw Violet go.

Step after shaky step. Her crying softened, but did not stop. She had resolved herself that she will make it to Westfairland or die trying.

King Roland was walking around the small village looking for any one that might need help in the festival preparations. He felt an odd intensity in his chest. It was his heart, he knew. He dismissed the sensation thinking it was just the excitement for the upcoming festival. It had been so long since Westfairland had a celebration, much less a reason to celebrate. Surely, he didn't feel nervous about meeting Trailynn.

He paused when he noticed a commotion among the fairies. Violet in the center of a small circle frantically speaking to the gathering. He felt a jolt at seeing Violet. He knew that she was supposed to be bringing Trailynn to Westfairland. Looking about the group as he approached, hoping to spot Trailynn before meeting her. When he didn't see the expected new face, he began to listen to what Violet was saying.

"Oh no!" King Roland yelled. "Trailynn!" Before anyone could stop him, King Roland ran into the tunnel calling out her name.

Violet went after him, to stop him. He would not be able to see in the darkness any better than Trailynn. Plus, he had not been out of Westfairland once since he first arrived. Great, she thought, now we have two humans to rescue!

Queen Gemeenah touched her shoulder to stop her. Violet looked at her inquisitively.

"Let him go. Then, follow behind him at a slight distance. Take a few fairies with you. Give him just enough light to make sure he does not run head first into a wall. Guide him if he starts down a wrong path. This is something that he needs to do." Queen Gemeenah said gently.

Violet nodded even though she did not understand. The group that helped bring the cookie baskets were standing ready. They also heard the Queen's words.

A few moments later, the group followed King Roland, lagging behind a bit as the Queen suggested.

As King Roland was running, he noticed the odd sensation in his chest grew slightly stronger. Suddenly, he remembered the last time he felt this way. It had been when he first laid eyes upon his beloved Isadora. He remembered that long-ago day with fondness. With the memory came knowledge.

King Roland had to acknowledge to himself how deeply he had grown to care for Trailynn. He also knew that all he had to do to find her was to follow his heart. This was all he needed. He ran forward even faster yelling her name.

Trailynn heard someone calling her name faintly. She couldn't orient herself to follow the voice at first. The walkways seemed to echo every sound in every direction. She stopped to really focus on the sound of her name. It was a man's voice. Not lilting like a fairy. Strong. It's King Roland! She just knew it. His voice became the only sound she could hear. The path she needed to take became clear in her mind's eye or was it her heart? She didn't know. She didn't care. She just knew that she would be saved and safe once they found each other.

Time was impossible to track. Neither knew how long they had been hurtling towards each other. Trailynn fell to her knees. He was close, knew felt. She was still surrounded by so much darkness.

"Trailynn?" King Roland whispered hoarsely. His voice strained from calling out for so long. He could see no better than she. His eyes had become accustomed to gem light long ago. He was still following the strange tightness in his heart. He sensed that he was getting close to her.

"Trailynn?" King Roland whispered again. The name had a hint of despair.

"I'm here!" Trailynn cried. "I'm here! Who has come to my rescue? Did Violet send you?"

"No, not really. I heard that you were lost in the tunnels and I couldn't bear the thought. I ran into the darkness to find you. I need to find you! I need to save you!" King Roland called back.

"But who are you?" Trailynn hoped it was King Roland, but didn't dare to say so, not out loud.

"It is I, King Roland!" he yelled, now his voice full of amusement. She was near.

"Oh! My dearest! I'm on the ground of this horrible tunnel. I cannot see a thing! Not even my own hands or feet! How will you ever find me? And when you do, how will we ever get out of here?" Trailynn's distress had eased knowing that King Roland was close. She thought, "Well, at least I won't die alone in this stupid tunnel!"

"AAAAAHHHHH!!!" Trailynn screamed in terror as something touched her hand. She thought of a million different horrible creatures that could be coming to finish her before King Roland saved her.

"Shh! It's me! I've found you!" King Roland had fallen to his knees in a crawl. He thought this way he was bound to find her since she was also on the floor of the tunnel. "Please, take my hand."

Trailynn waved her arms a bit in the darkness in front of her and suddenly grasped his hand. Then worked her way up his arms until she found his shoulders. Impulsively, she threw her arms around his neck. She clutched him to her tightly. Tears continued to flow. Now, her tears were of relief. Then her tears became those of happiness. She was about to pull away and apologize. What a forward thing to do? But King Roland held her just as tightly. He gave her a bit of a squeeze to let her know that he wasn't ready to let her go.

There, no longer alone in the darkness, wrapped in each other's arms, they knew everything would be all right. Trailynn turned her head slightly to whisper something in his ear.

"I, too, rushed headlong into the tunnel. I did so to find you." She softly whispered.

As she did so, the tears on their cheeks blended together causing a slight warming, glow. Neither knew what it meant at first. When they pulled apart slightly and opened their eyes, each was shocked because they could see. The darkness was still there, but they could see the other clearly.

"How can I see you now, my dearest?" Trailynn mumbled in confusion.

"I live in a cavern with fairies. I stopped asking those kinds of questions ages ago. I just learned to accept and go with it." King Roland replied with a small laugh. "I knew you would be beautiful. I must say though, you are far more beautiful than I could have possibly imagined." His voice taking on a hint of wonder.

Violet and the others who had remained back far enough for them to witness the interaction, but not close enough to hear. She did not need to hear a word. She now understood the Queen's instructions. King Roland and Trailynn had fallen deeply in love through their letter exchange. In love with their words, their minds, and, well, each other. It was the magic of love that allowed them to see each other so clearly.

Violet then mused to herself. The Queen misses nothing.

Chapter Thirty Six

The fairies had flown them close to the entrance of the cavern and then left them to finish the journey together. King Roland and Trailynn walked into the cavern together a few minutes later. Trailynn was no longer afraid. They had chatted the entire way, much to the amusement of their flight crew.

"Welcome to Westfairland!" King Roland waved his arm to gesture the expanse of the entire kingdom as a guide for Trailynn's eyes to follow.

Trailynn gasped at the sight before her. Fairies and humans of every color were everywhere. Laughing, talking, and just simply being. There were flowers, berry bushes, fruit trees. She took in the canal of fresh water with the small bridge. Houses like none that she had never seen. It was truly a fantastical array of life!

For the second time that day, Trailynn had no words.

"May I have the honor of showing you around?" King Roland gallantly offered his arm.

Trailynn smiled and bowed a little before taking his offered arm. She nodded and smiled in acknowledgement of each introduction. She knew better than to attempt to remember all the names of everyone that she was introduced to. There were so many it was almost overwhelming her.

She saw Queen Gemeenah across the bridge in deep conversation with a small heavily jeweled small man. Queen Gemeenah waved to her as a welcoming hello.

"Who is the Queen speaking to?" Trailynn asked.

"King Minegard. He is the King of the closest dwarf clan. He has been a very good friend. I'll introduce you when we get closer."

"MMMOOOOOMMMM!" Ilove yelled as she came running up to Trailynn. She flung her arms around her mother. "Isn't this the most amazing place? There are more people here than I have ever seen before. The witches arrived a little while ago. They are fabulous! You have to meet them!" Ilove's excitement at seeing her mother in Westfairland was overflowing.

"I will be happy to meet them. Can I wait a bit? King Roland has been very gracious in showing me around and making introductions. There is no way that I am going to remember anyone's name! And yes, this place is mind blowingly amazing! I understand completely why you want to come here so much!" Trailynn exclaimed as she returned Ilove's hug.

"It's more than just the people, Mom. I belong here." Ilove muttered. It was the first time she had admitted that to anyone. She had always been afraid to do so. She didn't quite understand why.

King Roland got called away on some official business. He was loath to he had to leave Trailynn, but duty first. It's all he has ever known. Trailynn assured him that she would be all right. She felt there was nothing and no one to fear in Westfairland. She marveled at how comfortable she felt being there.

As she moved through the community, she met several people of several different races, in awe at it all. She smiled at the snippets of conversations she overheard. Seemingly bizarre topics were commonplace here. She, also took advantage of the opportunity to observe her daughter in this environment. She came to realize the truth of Ilove's words. Ilove did belong here. This thought stabbed the core of Trailynn's heart.

Should she just let Ilove stay? How would she find any peace or happiness or love without her? Could she insist that Ilove stay with her just for her own selfish reasons? Deep in these thoughts, her face reflected her dilemma.

"Gold for your thoughts?" King Mineguard asked, interrupting her reverie.

"Oh! I'm sorry. Hello. I'm Ilove's mother, Trailynn. I was quite lost in my thoughts, wasn't I?" Trailynn blushed at being caught.

"Hello. My name is King Mineguard. I am King of the dwarf kingdom just west of here. It is a few mountains over. I am sorry to bother. You appeared quite sad for such a joyous occasion. There was a time when these festivals were held once a year. That turned into every few months. There was a human named Roman that would venture the world. He would come back with curious trinkets and interesting tales of the above world. I confess I am most pleased to be attending a Westfairland festival once again. May I ask what saddens you so?"

"Ilove. She is happier here than I have ever seen her before. What am I to do? She tells me that she truly belongs here. Seeing her here, I cannot disagree. I would gladly let her stay to let her live a happy life, but then I would at the same time, condemn myself to a life of misery without her." Trailynn paused to suppress a sob. "I am sorry to burden you with my thoughts."

"Alas, my lady, I understand more than you know. My son Prince Vander, left my kingdom to explore the world. I tried to discourage him. I warned him of the cruelty of humans. Present company excluded, of course." It was King Minegard's turn to blush. "Perhaps he was inspired by Roman. I do not know. He is now King Vander. A king in his own right. Hearing that makes me quite proud, though I miss him terribly."

"A king? He was clearly born to rule. I am sure he learned much from you. Where is his dwarf kingdom? I imagine that he found another kingdom in need of a king? Surely, he did not establish an entire kingdom on his own." Trailynn thought aloud.

'Oh, no. Honestly, I wish that were the situation. He was captured by a clan of giants. He was on the menu you see. While he was waiting to hit the cookpot, he overhead the giants discussing their ongoing feud with another clan. It seems that his captors were on the losing end of the feud. Warcraft is something all kings must study. Vander proposed a plan for the giants to defeat their enemies.

He bargained that if they won the battle using his plan then they would let him go. His plan worked, but the giants refused to let him go. Instead, they made him an advisor to their King. Soon every decision the King had to make Vander had to approve. The King grew angry and jealous of Vander. On the night before a big battle, the biggest battle that was meant to end the war, the King refused to follow Vander's plan.

He devised how own battle plan to prove that he could be just as successful and the better King. He was not. Many giants died that day, including the King. The remaining giants named Vander their new King. He had proven his ability to rule countless times. The clan is now the most successful and peaceful clan among all the giants."

"Wow! No wonder you are so proud! What an accomplishment!" Trailynn exclaimed. "He must be very pleased with himself to have gone out in the world to find so much success."

"Alas, no. He is miserable. He is happy with his accomplishments, but he is in love with a giantess. She returns his love, but they can never marry. He is a dwarf and she is a giantess." King Mineguard's cheeks redden as he gave Trailynn a sly, knowing look.

"That surprises me! I wouldn't think that race would be an issue here." Trailynn commented. "Why would it be forbidden?"

"Oh, no! Race is not the issue. Love is love. The issue with Vander and his beloved is… well….logistics!" King Mineguard replied, this time he was desperately attempting to avoid eye contact with Trailynn.

Trailynn's expression went from one of deep thought to utter shock and embarrassment as she finally understood the meaning words. "I see." was all that she was able to say while also avoiding eye contact.

"My point is that you will know what to do when the time comes. You may not like the options, but you will survive. I steadfastly refuse to believe that you will be doomed to despair! All will work out as it should." This time King Mineguard gave Trailynn a conspiratorial wink. He had witnessed how King Roland doted on her. He also noted that none of the magical peoples at the festival had any objections to her.

It also did not escape King Mineguard that both King Roland and Trailynn kept at track of each other even when they were engaged with other people. He could see the unspoken love between them. He knew that she would be one of the human exceptions to the magical world.

The festival continued well into the night. No one seemed to notice. Everyone was either eating, dancing, or laughing. There was story telling in a small niche by the bridge. The witches were entertaining groups with streamer lights and glitter birds. The dwarves were showing off their metalcraft techniques. There was no itinerary. Events just evolved organically. Trailynn marveled over the lack of any kind of strife. Again, she acknowledged to herself why Ilove preferred life in Westfairland. Now, she realized that she agreed. She would very much like living her as well.

King Roland approached Trailynn with his hand out. She intuitively clasped his hand. Both smiled at the other and blushed before looking away.

"I would be very interested in your thoughts." King Roland said.

"I have had many, many thoughts today. I understand why Ilove loves it here so much. I think that she will soon ask permission to stay. My heart is a bit heavy because I will let her. Her happiness is everything to me. She is right. She does belong here. I mean not just because she is your daughter's descendent. I mean I know she is part fairy. I just mean that... well... look at her. She has blossomed here. At home, in school... well... all things top world. Is that what you say? Top world?" Trailynn was rambling. "She is like an empty shell there and here she is all cheer. She is full of... well... light. I will miss her horribly."

King Roland turned to face Trailynn. He took in her beauty. He saw the mixture of elation and sadness in her eyes. Every little nuance about her moved his heart.

"Would you have any interest in staying here as well? I know people. I could try to make that happen, if you want." It was King Roland's turn to stumble over a mouth full of words. So much to say. He laughed nervously when she didn't get his joke. "I mean... would you ever want to live in Westfairland? With Ilove?" Now for the really brave bit. "With me?"

King Roland stared at his shoes like it was the first time seeing them. His shoes were suddenly the most captivating things he had ever beheld. He mustered the courage to ask her to stay with him, but not the courage to see her reaction. Was she pleased? Eager? Horrified? The silence seemed to drag.

"Is that possible?" Trailynn found her voice once she had a moment to reflect on his words. "I thought there was a committee or something and all humans had to be accepted by all races. I wouldn't want to put Ilove...or you in a bad spot." So much was being said to each other without actually saying the right words. Each understood though. Both wanted to stay with the other. Both knew they loved each other. Neither was prepared to profess it yet.

"Ah, don't be mad. I didn't mean to presume anything, but I… um… already asked about it." King Roland softly touched her face, guiding her to look at him. "I asked permission to invite you to stay with Ilove. The truth is though I want to ask you to stay with me." King Roland paused to release the breath he didn't know he was holding. "I don't mean for you to move in with me or anything like that. I'm not that presumptuous. That would be most improper. But I would very much like it if you were to move to Westfairland so that I may court you properly."

No words could express her racing thoughts. Instead, Trailynn leaned slightly on her toes to give King Roland the sweetest kiss. Historians and poets could write volumes about that kiss.

There was nothing more that needed to be said.

Part Three

Ever After

Chapter Thirty Seven

Trailynn went home to pack up her house. She went to town to spread news that she was moving away to be closer to family. She sold the cottage and used the funds to settle all her accounts. She didn't want any one in the village to have any reason to come looking for them after the move.

Queen Gemeenah had a dwelling constructed for her on the opposite side of the cavern from King Roland. The house was close to Edward's and she thought it would be a good place for the Kingstons to settle. Fairies and witches alike helped Trailynn with the move. The worked at night to as a measure against prying eyes. On the last day in her former home, she looked around and felt overcome with memories. Her heart was full of excitement for the future. She was experiencing a delightful mix of sadness at leaving behind everything familiar and happiness for the life that will be filled with unknown wonders.

It didn't take long for Trailynn to find her footing in Westfairland. She loved the little house that she shared with Ilove. She wanted for nothing. King Roland was true to his word, he relished in courting her. The two continued to write to each other. Only now, they wrote sweet missives instead of letters. Each day was a new gift.

Ilove had never been happier. Violet took on the role of teacher. She taught Ilove fairy ways and worked with her on exploring her fairy gifts. Azure and Cloven continued to travel top side. The humans would see vibrantly dancing dragonflies. On occasions, they would choose to travel by light so that Ilove could go exploring with them. Other days, Ilove would spend with Edward learning his woodcraft. She mostly just observed, but always offered a helping hand. The joy was in the companionship, not necessarily the work.

One very fine day King Roland came to Edward's workshop seeking Ilove. He found her sitting on a bench that Edward had made for her.

"Hello, Ilove. May I sit? I have missed the talks we used to have." King Roland said.

"Of course. It has been a minute since we had a talk. Now, I feel like I have neglected you. I just figured that you already knew how my day is going. It's not like it was with me in the human world. You already know how I spend my days." Ilove replied.

King Roland sat next to Ilove. He was so nervous. He knew he had no reason to be but still….

"So are you liking Westfairland? Do you like it as much as you thought you would?" he queried.

Ilove took a moment to answer. He is acting strange Ilove thought to herself. Hmm…. Something is up.

"Out with it?" Ilove exclaimed.

"What?" King Roland was caught completely off guard. He forgot how perceptive and direct she could be. Shaking his head with a small laugh, "Why would something be up? I just came to chat."

He glanced at Ilove to catch her knowing expression on her face. She needed no words. Her face said it all.

"Okay. Okay. Okay." King Roland relinquished with his hands up. "Something is on my mind that I wanted to discuss with you. I want to know how you would feel if I asked for your mother's hand." He paused for a small intake of air. "For marriage." He gave Ilove a barely noticeable sideway glance. He dared so say nothing more.

"Are you asking me for permission? Done." Ilove gently touched his hand to get his attention. She wanted him to face her, to see her face, to see her sincerity. "I believe my mother is happier now here with you than she has ever been. I have no memories of my mother with my father. I was a baby when he was sent to war. She told me all about him, told me many stories. How they met. Their time together. And she never once looked as happy reliving those memories as she is with you. I don't mean to suggest that she didn't love my father. I know she did. But you. If there is any truth to soulmates or true love, that is what you are to my mother. I would be honored to call you dad."

King Roland was moved by her words. He wouldn't speak. Couldn't speak. He knew that if he tried his emotions would get away from him. Instead, he simply nodded and hugged her before taking his leave of her.

"Well, that was quite a thing to see." Edward said.

Ilove just smiled in reply.

Chapter Thirty Eight

The day of the wedding had arrived.

Trailynn would not have believed that any celebration could have topped the very first festival that she attended in Westfairland. She was wrong.

There had never been a royal wedding in Westfairland. All the magical peoples came. Many Trailynn had met before. She thrilled at the new faces. Always something or some new these days. She reflected back to her days at the cottage. She lived a small quiet life. She was content. Never could she has dreamed her life now. Getting married. To a king!

"Uh hmm." Marigold cleared her throat to get Trailynn's attention. "I came to help you finish getting ready. It is almost time."

Trailynn's wedding dress was standing in the corner of her room. How she didn't know. She had come to understand King Roland's words when they first met. Don't ask. Just go with it.

The dress was beyond stunning. Both fairies and witches had a hand in crafting the dress for her. The fitted bodice and sleeves were fine cream colored silk. The dress flowed down to her hips where it started to flare out. Flowering vines began at the hem covering the skirt. Small delicate flowers of every color. Exquisite. It was the only word that she could think of.

"Oh! Thank you! I was just thinking that I cannot believe I get to wear such a beautiful dress."

Queen Gemeenah came in a few minutes later. She held Iadore's daisy crown on a pillow.

"I believe this will complete your outfit." She said.

"I couldn't possibly wear this." Trailynn stammered. "It's too much. This was Iadore's. I just couldn't."

"You can. You should. I checked with King Roland and he is in agreement. This crown is now yours. Unless as Queen, you would like your own crown. You have that right." Queen Gemeenah explained.

"Queen? Me? My own crown?" Trailynn couldn't believe the words she was hearing. How had she missed the fact that she would be a queen?

"That is what happens when you marry a king, my dear." Queen Gemeenah was amused and pleased. She never once thought that Trailynn was marrying King Roland to be a queen. This confirmation of that knowledge.

Queen Gemeenah handed the pillow to Marigold. Then she placed the crown on Trailynn's head. "There. Finishing touch."

Trailynn looked at herself in the mirror. Stunned by the sight of herself.

"Well, only one thing left to do." Trailynn giggled. "I guess it's time."

"I guess it is." Queen Gemeenah answered.

Queen Gemeenah walked out first. She signaled for everyone to take the place as she took hers in the middle of the small bridge. A trail of bluebells sprouted up along the path she took. Moments later the bluebells began to play a sweet song. This was the cue for King Roland and Trailynn to begin their own procession to the bridge. He came from one side of Westfairland. She came from the other. Each had to come halfway to meet in the middle.

Queen Gemeenah performed the uniting ceremony.

"Welcome all. We have come here today to witness and celebrate the joining of King Roland to Trailynn Kingston." Queen Gemeenah then turned to King Roland. "King Roland of Westfairland, do you take Trailynn Kingston to be your bride and your queen?"

"I absolutely do. Today and every day for the rest of my life." King Roland gushed with his eyes brimming with unshed tears of love and joy.

Turning to Trailynn Queen Gemeenah continued. "Trailynn Kingston, do you take King Roland of Westfairland to be your husband and your king?"

"I do. I do. I do." Trailynn's happiness could not be bound. Her tears flowed gently down her cheeks. "A thousand times, I do."

"With great honor it is my privilege to pronounce you husband and wife. King and Queen of Westfairland." Giving King Roland a slight nod. "You may kiss your bride."

King Roland leaned in to Trailynn. He touched her face and whispered, "I love you, wife." Sweetly, he kissed her.

"I love you too, husband."

King Roland and Queen Trailynn were lost to each other.

"Let the celebration begin!" Queen Gemeenah declared.

The End